BOOK THIRTY

The magician glanced at Carolyn, his eyes aglitter with hatred. She felt a cold chill as he stared at her. Then with no warning at all he abruptly seized her and in a second had her on her knees before the guillotine, her head through the opening. She was too shocked to struggle until that instant, but by then it was too late. She heard him jerk the lever and felt the deadly blade drop down to decapitate her!

Hermes Press

Published by Hermes Press, an imprint of
Herman and Geer Communications, Inc.

Daniel Herman, Publisher
Kandice Hartner, Production Manager/Sr. Graphic Designer
Eileen Sabrina Herman, Managing Editor
Erica McNatt, Copy Editor/Graphic Designer
Jake Merkel, Graphic Designer
Brian Peck, Special Projects Editor

2100 Wilmington Road
Neshannock, Pennsylvania 16105
(724) 652-0511
www.HermesPress.com; info@hermespress.com

Book design by Eileen Sabrina Herman
First printing, 2023

LCCN applied for: 10 9 8 7 6 5 4 3 2 1 0
ISBN 978-1-61345-257-8
OCR and text editing by H + G Media and Eileen Sabrina Herman
Proof reading by Eileen Sabrina Herman and Fey McKinley

From Dan, Sabrina, and Jacob in memory of Al DeVivo

Acknowledgments: This book would not be possible without the help and encouragement of Jim Pierson and Curtis Holdings

Printed in China

Barnabas, Quentin and the Mad Magician
by Marilyn Ross

CONTENTS

CHAPTER 1

"Isn't it exciting?" Carolyn Stoddard's tone revealed awe as she stared down at the strange procession winding its way along the narrow private road to Kerrhaven, the impressive three-story Victorian mansion on the estate next to Collinwood.

"So Cabrini has arrived at last!" Beth Mayberry exclaimed. She was a pretty, dark girl of Carolyn's age, and while her parents were in Japan on business she was spending the summer vacation period at Collinwood as a guest of her school friend.

The two girls were standing on a hillside which overlooked the adjoining estate and so had an excellent view of the motor caravan slowly moving down the road a distance below them. From their vantage point the trucks and cars looked like toy models.

It was sunset of a pleasant, warm June evening, and the two girls in their attractive print dresses had no hint of what the arrival of the caravan of the world-famous European magician, Cabrini, would mean to Collinsport and its people. Neither of them guessed that it would be Black Magic the noted Cabrini would introduce to the area. And that before the summer had ended strange phantoms would walk the night, terrifying events would occur, and some of those alive at that moment would die in a macabre fashion!

A large black limousine led the caravan. It was followed by three huge moving vans, and the procession wound up with a large, blue station wagon. It moved along the road toward the cliffs where the ancient green mansion with its white-trimmed bay windows stood along with the numerous outbuildings attached to the place. There was also the cottage, a distance from the main house, in which the owners of the estate, William Kerr and his sister, Adele, now lived. Soon after purchasing the property they had moved into the cottage and rented the main buildings whenever they could. William Kerr was a wealthy blind man whose hobby was writing poetry, and his spinster sister, Adele, looked after his household. They traveled a great deal and spent only a few weeks at Kerrhaven in any given year.

The balance of the time the main building was rented to summer residents or was simply left empty. The estate had a year-round caretaker whom Carolyn knew only as Irving. She was not certain whether this was his first or last name. He was a gnarled, dour man who suffered from deafness but seemed to manage well enough in taking care of the place. Like the other young people in the area, Carolyn had always been a little afraid of the old man, and so she avoided Kerrhaven when the Kerrs weren't at home.

When the blind, gentle William Kerr and his plain but friendly sister Adele were there it was a different matter. Carolyn, her mother and her Uncle Roger were frequently guests at the cottage for tea or dinner. And a warm friendship had developed between the Kerrs and her family. As it happened the Kerrs were now living at the cottage and only a few days earlier had been Elizabeth's guests for dinner at Collinwood. Afterward as they all sat in the living room, the white-haired, slightly-stooped poet had spoken of renting Kerrhaven to the magician.

In his pleasant, quiet fashion he said, "I'm sure you've all read of the noted European magician, Cabrini. I have had the privilege of knowing him personally. And this summer he is coming to stay at Kerrhaven and work on the production for his first American tour. He has a large staff and builds huge, fantastic illusions for his theater shows."

Young David Collins, who had been seated on a stool by the fireplace, at once stood up eagerly. "Is he the one who makes a girl float on stage and then vanish over the audience?"

The frail, white-haired man with the black glasses smiled. "That is one of his famous illusions, David. I have never seen it done, of course, but Adele has described it to me."

His plain, elderly sister seemed excited. "It's true," she said. "It was one of the most amazing illusions I've ever seen. But then, the entire evening was full of thrills."

William Kerr nodded. "From all I've been told Cabrini is greater than Blackstone, Thurston or even Houdini. He's considered the top magician overseas today."

From his stand by the fireplace Roger Collins spoke up in his dry fashion. "I think Collinsport could do without such an exotic character. We've had too much excitement here. I prefer to see the ordinary run-of-the-mill tourist come here."

Elizabeth Stoddard, seated near him, glanced at her brother. "I think you're wrong, Roger," she reproved him. "I say it's wonderful having Cabrini here. I only wish he'd do a special outdoor show here at Collinwood for the Collinsport hospital fund."

The blind poet said, "I'm sure that can be arranged. I'll ask him as soon as he arrives."

Elizabeth's attractive, matronly face took on a pleased look. "How kind of you, William. How wonderful it would be for us all!"

David gazed at his Aunt Elizabeth with a too-good-to-be-true expression. "Then I'd be able to see the whole show right here," he said.

"We should be able to sell hundreds of tickets," Elizabeth said.

"I agree," Carolyn joined in enthusiastically.

Only the reserved Roger Collins had a cold attitude toward the project. "What sort of person is this Cabrini?" he wanted to know. "And what are the people working with him like? Is his staff liable to give the town police any trouble?"

The poet sat up in his chair, his thin hands grasping the arms tensely. "From all I know about Cabrini and his work I'd venture to say the members of his company will all be of fine reputation."

Roger frowned. "I hope so. They'll be right next to us. The idea of having a lot of strangers around is worrisome."

Elizabeth gave her brother a reproving glance. "I'm sure William has always been careful about who he's rented his property to. The people who have rented Kerrhaven in the past have been most desirable."

"Thank you," the blind man said quietly. "I do try to screen the rental applicants. And Adele makes it a rule to interview them before ever accepting them as tenants."

"That is so," Adele agreed. "In several instances I turned down dubious applicants for the house. It's not as if we must have it rented."

"I know that," Elizabeth said.

"My reason for renting to Cabrini is our friendship of course," William Kerr explained. "And I think the house and outbuildings ideal for his purpose. He found it impractical to bring his larger illusions across the ocean with him. This means his chief carpenter and assistants must recreate them over here. The huge barn will make an ideal workshop and rehearsal theater."

"Is he an old man?" Carolyn asked.

The blind poet smiled. "Some few years younger than myself. But he is well-preserved for his years. He has an imposing personality. You will like him."

David said enthusiastically, "It's the greatest! We'll really have something happening in Collinsport this year."

"As long as too much doesn't happen," his father said.

"I think Cabrini will add color to the summer community," the blind man told them. "There will be a lot of stories in the newspapers about his being here and preparing for the tour. And it should arouse interest on the part of tourists. A lot of people may travel here just to see his headquarters."

"How long does he plan to stay?" Carolyn asked.

"At least until early September," William Kerr said. "In the meantime he'll be building and rehearsing the show, and I haven't a doubt he'll stage a charity performance for you, Elizabeth."

"The hospital fund can use the money," Carolyn's mother said.

David was wide-eyed. "Can Cabrini really do things by magic or is it all a lot of tricks?"

The white-haired man laughed softly. "I must admit a great deal of trickery is involved. Still, those who have seen him insist that he has more than mere sleight-of-hand skill. Some say he truly has magical powers, and it is well known that he is an expert hypnotist."

"I do not approve of stage hypnotism," was Roger Collins' caustic comment. "I consider it far too risky to tamper with people's minds for the mere purpose of entertaining the ignorant and curious."

"As far as I know, Cabrini is extremely careful in using his hypnotic prowess," the poet said. "I agree with you that hypnotism can be dangerous under certain conditions."

"It should only be used by competent medical men," Roger said.

Adele Kerr nodded. "I quite agree. But I have an idea I read somewhere that Cabrini has some medical training."

"True," her brother said. "Cabrini studied to be a doctor but did not quite complete his course. After that he turned to a career as a professional stage magician. So he must fully understand the medical aspect of hypnotism."

Elizabeth looked interested. "He must be a most unusual man."

"I can promise you that," William Kerr assured her.

And then the talk had moved on to other things. But from that night on Carolyn had eagerly looked forward to the arrival of the magician. The weeks seemed to drag by with discouraging slowness. When Beth Mayberry came to Collinwood for the holidays Carolyn told her about Cabrini's promised arrival, and they speculated on how much excitement it would cause.

And now on this June evening the big moment had arrived. The girls stood on the hill watching the line of cars and trucks wind its way toward Kerrhaven.

Carolyn turned to her friend and said, "We must go back to Collinwood and tell my mother."

"And David," Beth said with a smile. "He's the one who'll be the most delighted."

Carolyn glanced toward the disappearing caravan again and said, "I wouldn't be surprised if he were somewhere down there now. He's always the first to know about these things."

With that they turned and headed back down the other side of the hill toward Collinwood. The sun was setting with its background of gold, crimson, and finally gray. The air was warm with a tang of the nearby salty ocean. Directly ahead of them, perched high on the cliffs overlooking Collinsport Bay, was the dark, sprawling Collinwood mansion. Behind the big main house were the stables, barns and other buildings. Far to the left, partially hidden by evergreens, was the original home of the Collins family, which dated back to the end of the eighteenth century.

"I can hardly wait to go down and meet Cabrini and his company," Carolyn said to her friend as they walked along. "Do you suppose they have girls in the company?"

The dark-haired, pretty Beth considered. "I'd expect so. Most magicians have girl assistants in ridiculously short skirts. At least all I've seen had them."

"We'll soon know," Carolyn predicted with a smile as they crossed the broad lawn leading to the front entrance of Collinwood. "Maybe we can get a job with the show?"

Beth's black eyes came impishly alive. "I'd jump at the chance!"

"Your parents might have something to say about that," Carolyn warned her friend.

"They won't be back for months."

Carolyn sighed. "I'd like to be in a show like that myself. But even if mother would agree I'm positive Uncle Roger wouldn't allow it."

"He can be stubborn," Beth agreed. "I've noticed that."

"And suspicious of everyone," Carolyn said with a sigh. "He was the longest time becoming friendly with the Kerrs after they bought the estate next to us. And even now he doesn't approve of them fully. I'm sure he's annoyed at their renting the house to Cabrini and his company."

They had reached the front door of Collinwood, and Carolyn led the way inside. In the living room they found Elizabeth and Roger talking. The two older people turned to the girls as they entered the room.

"Cabrini is here," Carolyn said, all excitement.

Elizabeth raised her eyebrows. "Are you sure?"

"We saw the caravan of trucks and cars, Mrs. Stoddard," Beth said.

Roger's stern face revealed a slight annoyance. "So they've finally come," he observed dourly. "I'd hoped Cabrini might change his mind."

"I'm glad they've come," Carolyn exulted. "The whole village has been so dead. We need some excitement!"

Roger observed her with disdain. "The kind of excitement he may bring may not be the sort we want."

Elizabeth waved aside his remark with a quick gesture. "Don't be so stuffy, Roger. I fully agree with Carolyn. And I know David will be thrilled. I wonder where he is?"

Carolyn said, "I have an idea he may be down at Kerrhaven watching the caravan come in."

Her uncle glared at her. "I hope not. If he is there I'll have a few things to say to him when he gets back."

Carolyn pouted. "I think you're being mean about this, Uncle Roger. You're spoiling the fun for us."

Elizabeth gave her daughter a warning look. "Be careful, my dear."

Carolyn refused to be quiet. "I don't care, mother. I mean it. I think Uncle Roger is being too narrow-minded. You'd think the Collins family never had a skeleton in its closet. And we all know better than that!"

Roger's face was crimson now. Hands clenched, he came up to face her. "Just what are you implying by that?"

But she wasn't going to back down. "You know the stories about Collinwood as well as I do. You've heard about the ghosts and the witches!"

"Ignorant village gossip," her uncle rasped.

"Maybe," Carolyn said. "But down through the years lots of mysterious things have happened in this house. Things that can't be explained. And at least some of the family fortune was made out of the slave trade!"

Roger stared at her in wordless rage and then turned to Elizabeth in a fury. Pointing a finger at Carolyn, he asked, "Did you hear what your daughter said just now?"

Elizabeth looked shaken but she didn't lose poise. Calmly she said, "I'm afraid the family history bears out her story. Not that I approve of her dwelling on it." And to Carolyn, she said, "You must remember that for more than a century the Collins name has been a most honored one."

"Maybe," Carolyn said. "But what about Quentin Collins?"

"We do not speak of Quentin in this house," Roger warned her.

Carolyn smiled coolly. "I guess that's because you don't dare. And what about Barnabas? Barnabas, who is my friend. I suppose you don't want his name mentioned here either."

Roger snapped, "If your mother is foolish enough to allow you to be friendly with Barnabas that is her affair. For myself, I can only wish that he never returns here again. He does not belong to our branch of the family."

"He is still a cousin, even though he lives in England," Carolyn pointed out.

Roger said, "I've revealed my feelings. Not that they seem to have much importance in this house anymore." And to Elizabeth, he said, "I leave it to you to discipline this unruly young lady." With that he stalked out of the room.

When he was safely out of the way Carolyn's mother gave her a despairing glance, and asked, "How could you upset Roger so? And in front of Beth as well."

"I didn't mind," Beth spoke up.

Elizabeth looked at her with troubled eyes. "I'm sure you must have been embarrassed no matter what you say. You are our guest and shouldn't be subjected to family bickerings. Carolyn knows better than to talk as she did."

Carolyn sighed. "I'm sorry."

"You should be," her mother said. "And it was very wrong of you to drag Quentin and Barnabas into the conversation. Especially Cousin Barnabas who has been so kind to you."

"I was just trying to let Roger know how bigoted he is," Carolyn protested.

"That's not the way to handle your uncle," Elizabeth said. "All you did was make trouble for Barnabas. And surely he has enough. You must learn to be more considerate."

"Very well," Carolyn said unhappily.

Elizabeth turned to Beth. "We want you to enjoy your stay here. Just try and pretend you didn't hear any of this."

"That will be easy," the pretty girl promised.

"I hope so," Elizabeth sighed. And she also left the room.

After a minute of their being in the room by themselves, Beth came over to Carolyn and said, "You hit on all the wrong things. We'll be lucky now if we're ever given permission to visit Kerrhaven."

"We can go without permission."

"Would you?"

"If I wanted to."

The other girl looked slightly anxious as she considered this. "I don't know," she worried. "Your uncle sounded awfully angry."

"He'll get over it. He always does."

"Who are the two you mentioned?" Beth asked. "Quentin and Barnabas."

Carolyn sighed. "Just two of the more interesting members of our family. But try and convince Roger or even mother of that. Though she's better than Uncle Roger."

"Did you say that Barnabas was English?"

"He belongs to that branch of the family," Carolyn said. "They've lived in England for centuries. He's a true gentleman, quite unlike Roger." There were also other things about the background of Barnabas which she knew but didn't feel like confiding to her friend.

"Does he come here often?"

Carolyn looked bleak. "Not as often as I'd like. He hasn't been here for months now. When he does come he stays at the old house. He had it restored for his personal use."

"The old brick house on the road to the cemetery? I thought it was closed," Beth said.

"We keep it closed unless Barnabas is here visiting," she explained. "A right was given him years ago to use the old house for as long as he lives. Then it reverts to the estate."

"Is that why Roger dislikes him so?" Beth asked.

"It might be one reason," Carolyn admitted. "According to the terms of one of the ancient wills the members of the English branch of the family have the use of the place. Barnabas is the only surviving member of the English group."

"And Quentin?" Beth said.

She made a face. "Another cousin. Very handsome and unfortunately very wild. He made a bad reputation for himself when he was here last. And yet he is likable."

"What did he do?"

Carolyn hesitated. She did not know how to properly explain to this friend about her handsome male cousins. It had taken her a good while to understand. And she knew about the dark shadows which hung over many of the members of the Collins family. The grim history of Collinwood had been drilled into her. But how to tell a stranger?

How could one explain that Quentin had been born under the curse of the werewolf and that at certain times of the moon he reverted to a primitive state? And would it be any easier to make the pretty dark girl understand that Barnabas was more than a century old and a vampire? That long ago, as the result of an unhappy romantic triangle, he had been bitten by a vampire bat and turned into one of the living dead!

If she tried to make such things seem reasonable to Beth surely she was doomed to failure. Either the dark-haired girl would doubt her or she'd be terrified of Quentin and Barnabas. The odd fact was that there was no need for her to become panic stricken. The appearance of Quentin or Barnabas gave no warning of their distorted lives. In most instances they were harmless and even helpful. At least Carolyn felt that way about Barnabas. She had never been entirely easy where Quentin was concerned.

Now Beth's voice came to her again, pressing the question a second time. "What did Quentin do when he was here last?"

Forcing herself to make some sort of reply, Carolyn said, "He became involved in a scandal. There was a murder not far away. He was one of the suspects."

"Was he guilty?"

"No. But for a time it seemed that he might be."

Beth looked puzzled. "If he were proven innocent why should Roger feel as he does about him?"

"Quentin makes him uneasy."

"I see," the other girl said. "And is this true of your British cousin, Barnabas?"

"Yes," Carolyn sighed. "Barnabas is much too complex a person for Uncle Roger to ever understand. Come out to the hall." And she led the way.

When they reached the shadowed hallway she pointed up at the portrait of a handsome, dark man with a gaunt, lean look. "That is a painting of the first Barnabas Collins. It was done before he left Maine for England two centuries ago. And the present holder of the name resembles his ancestor to a remarkable degree."

Beth studied the portrait. "He's very good-looking if he is anything like this painting."

"He could have sat for it," Carolyn said wryly. She couldn't dare attempt to make Beth believe the truth: Barnabas had sat for it. He was the one and only Barnabas Collins. He had wandered down through the centuries as a prowler of the night, one of the living dead doomed to the world of darkness.

Beth turned to her with a smile. "I'd like to meet your Barnabas."

"Perhaps you will," Carolyn said. "He often returns during the summer months."

"What does Roger say to that?"

"There's nothing he can say or do," Carolyn told the girl. "Barnabas has the old house for his use whenever he wants it."

Beth eyed her wisely. "I'm beginning to understand that life at Collinwood is not quite as simple an existence as I thought."

"You are so right," Carolyn said. "Let's walk across the lawn and see if we can find David. They'll worry about him if he doesn't return soon."

"All right," Beth agreed.

Outside, the blue haze of twilight hung over everything. The two girls strolled slowly in the direction of Kerrhaven talking quietly. There was an odd stillness in the air that might have meant rain. And yet it was more than a stillness; it was a strange kind of tension you could almost feel.

Suddenly Carolyn halted and pointed ahead in the darkness. "I think I see David running toward us," she said. And she called out, "Is that you, David?"

"Yes," came his reply in a voice that hinted of relief. And in a moment he came up to them. He was breathless as he gasped, "I saw Cabrini arrive. They're taking a lot of stuff into the barn. They're a real spooky lot. When they saw me they just stared at me and said nothing!"

"You shouldn't have gone there without permission," Carolyn warned him.

The boy looked up at them through the growing shadows. "You won't tell on me?"

"Not if you go straight home," Carolyn said.

"Where are you going?" he wanted to know.

"Just for a little walk," she said. "Your father is worried about you. You'll be in real trouble if you don't hurry home."

"I'm on my way," David promised. "Remember, don't tell where I was!" And he ran off in the darkness toward Collinwood.

Beth smiled at Carolyn. "Your guess about his being at Kerrhaven was right."

"I know him." Carolyn hesitated. "I suppose we should go back now that we've found him."

"Not yet."

"No?"

"No," Beth said in her impish way. "I'd like to walk as far as Kerrhaven. We can watch from the shadows without anyone seeing us."

Carolyn stared at her. "We'd be trespassing. Taking a chance."

"You're bound to be invited there anyhow," Beth protested. "What difference can it make?"

"We haven't been invited yet."

"But we will be," Beth insisted. "Let's go a little way at least."

Carolyn pondered. "I don't think it's a good idea," she told her friend. But she did begin to stroll slowly on. In spite of her uneasiness she was also curious about what was happening at the adjoining mansion.

So they walked down the hill to the road along which the caravan had come. It was completely dark now, a night without stars. They could barely find their way along the narrow road. Carolyn was experiencing regrets that she'd allowed her friend to influence her in this. Her every instinct warned her to turn and hurry back.

She was about to suggest this to Beth when they passed the final bend in the road and saw the lights of Kerrhaven ahead. There was a bustle of activity there; the lights of trucks were visible and unloading was going on. Loud voices echoed foreign words through the night as Cabrini's staff worked at moving the contents of the trucks into the barn.

Carolyn halted and said, "I think we've come far enough."

Beth touched her arm in the darkness. "It's exciting, isn't it? Can't we go just a little closer?"

"We shouldn't!"

"No one will notice us!" Beth argued in a loud whisper.

"We can't be sure!"

"Come on!" Beth insisted, taking her by the arm and urging her on.

Carolyn was now positive she'd made a grave error in coming at all. Beth was far too reckless. She'd not realized this before. The dark girl led her very close to the scene of the unloading. Lanterns had been set out at various points to illuminate the scene, and some of the men were using flashlights.

The workers were all of a foreign type, a lot of them swarthy-skinned and with jet black hair. They were mostly lithe young men who moved quickly and engaged in noisy badinage as they carried what appeared to be heavy trunks and wooden crates.

Beth leaned close to Carolyn and whispered, "They're taking everything into the barn."

And they were. Carolyn could see that. But all she could think of was getting away without their being seen. She felt they were intruders in a place where they weren't welcome. She was about to make a final attempt to urge Beth to leave when terror exploded around them.

Someone cried out angrily in a foreign language directly behind them, and the two startled girls turned to discover a weird and sinister figure holding one of the lanterns directly before them. He was a hunchback with a short black beard and a broad ugly face. He wore a black, soft hat sloped down to his eyes. And the eyes under it burned malevolently as he snarled at them again and reached out a hairy hand to snatch Carolyn by the arm!

CHAPTER 2

"No!" Carolyn drew back in terror from the bearded hunchback.

But she was not swift enough. He deftly seized her with his free hand and, grinning evilly, held the lantern up to examine her more closely. "What are you doing here?" he asked in an accented voice.

Before Carolyn could answer, Beth came forward in protest. "How dare you behave in this manner!" she chided the hunchback. "Let her go!"

He turned from Carolyn to the other girl with a derisive smile. "You have a fire in you, senorita," he said in his thick accent. "I like that!"

"Let my friend go!" Beth insisted.

The hunchback chuckled and released his cruel grip on Carolyn's arm. "You two have no right here," he informed them.

Carolyn spoke up, "We know that and we're sorry. But we are friends of Mr. Kerr and we felt sure you wouldn't mind."

"Cabrini does not like intruders," the hunchback said.

"We meant no harm," Beth assured him.

"That is true," Carolyn said. "We were just interested in seeing you unloading."

The ugly face of the hunchback showed disdain. "You can tell Cabrini about that," he said. And indicating the barn door with a nod, he added, "You will find him in there."

Carolyn was still frightened, and she didn't relish the idea of going into the dark barn. She said, "Must we bother him now? We'd much rather go back home."

"He has to know about your being here," the hunchback said harshly. "So you better go in and get it over with."

"You're making a great deal of something that isn't important," Carolyn told him.

He stood there, a bent, weird figure with the lantern showing off his black-bearded, ugly face. Those burning eyes were fixed on her as he said in his accented manner, "We'll let Cabrini decide that!"

Beth looked angry. She told Carolyn, "If we must go see this Cabrini let us get it over with!"

"I don't like it," Carolyn said uneasily. "He has no right to order us around this way."

"I suppose we are trespassers and spying on them," Beth said, with a sigh. "It will be easier to explain to Cabrini, I'm sure."

"Very well," Carolyn said, resigning herself to what was surely an awkward and unreasonable situation. She could imagine her Uncle Roger's reaction to all this.

Beth led the way to the barn door. The men working on the trucks were not taking anything directly into the barn for the moment but merely removing crates from the vans and placing them on the ground. The hunchback followed behind the two girls and stood with the lantern, waiting for them to enter the barn.

Carolyn turned to him to ask nervously, "Are you sure Cabrini is in there?"

The hunchback nodded. "You'll find him!"

She sighed and took a step into the darkness. At the far end of the barn there was a lantern hanging from a rafter to give a small amount of light. But the glow from it was confined to a tiny area revealing only a number of piled trunks and boxes. Otherwise the long, vaulted-roofed barn was in darkness.

Standing in the shadows with Beth at her side, she said in a low voice, "I don't see anyone. That hunchback must be mad!"

"He's surly enough!" Beth agreed.

Before Carolyn could answer, a fantastic thing happened. The barn rang with a shrill, mad laughter and a skeleton danced from the shadows. It thrust forward its grinning skull and dangled a bony hand. Both girls screamed with terror and drew back from the ghostly creature.

And then in a second the skeleton vanished, and a strong flashlight beam blinded them. They were confused and terrified. A deep male voice sounded from behind the flashlight. "What are you doing here?"

Frantically Carolyn gasped, "The hunchback sent us!"

"Chavez?" the voice asked.

"Whatever his name is," Carolyn said.

The flashlight shifted so that they were able to see over it. For the first time the tall, spare bald man holding the flashlight was revealed.

"I am Cabrini," he announced in his deep, impressive voice. His head was shaven completely bald and he had a stern, bony face. He bore a frightening resemblance to the skeleton which had just terrified them except his body was clothed in a tight-fitting black outfit.

Beth spoke up, "Your man, Chavez, insisted we come in here."

The tall man with the flashlight studied her with interest. His bald head seemed to float above them in the darkness. "Why?"

"We came here without invitation," Carolyn said. "He resented our watching the trucks unload."

Cabrini's deep-set hypnotic eyes fixed on her. "Are you not aware that magicians jealously preserve their privacy and their secrets? Chavez did not want you spying on us."

"We didn't intend to spy. We're friends of William Kerr, who owns this place," Carolyn said.

Cabrini at once looked less stern. "You are friends of William Kerr and his sister?"

"Yes," Carolyn said. "We are neighbors. I'm Carolyn Collins. My family owns Collinwood, the adjoining estate, and this is my friend, Beth Mayberry."

Cabrini stared at them in the darkness for a long moment and then he actually smiled. "In that case this has been an unfortunate error on the part of Chavez and myself. You will accept our apologies, I hope?"

Beth drew a sigh of relief. "I may accept your apology but I'll never forgive you for terrifying us with that skeleton thing."

The bald man in the black, knit sweater and tights continued to be amused at their plight. "That is a very useful bit of apparatus which I was just unpacking. I couldn't resist the temptation to try the illusion on you. Dramatic, isn't it?"

"I almost lost my heartbeat," Carolyn admitted.

"You scared us nearly to death," Beth said. "And it wasn't very kind of you."

"But I thought you were intruders," Cabrini said. "I had no idea Chavez had told you to come in here."

"Now you know," Beth told him.

The master magician shifted the blinding flashlight to study them more closely. He said, "I've offered my regrets. And later I hope that I may be able to have you here as my guests and really show you the place."

"We'll omit your skeleton trick next time," Beth told him.

Cabrini laughed. "Of course," he said. "Now I'll see you safely outside and explain to Chavez. His English is not too good and often he becomes confused. And always he is too cautious. You must forgive him."

"He's not an attractive person," Carolyn told the magician.

"I agree," Cabrini said. "But he is a master craftsman and an excellent assistant. I can ask no more."

Carolyn was beginning to feel a little less afraid. She still found the magician an awesome figure but he seemed less frightening now. And she realized that what he said about magicians needing to preserve their privacy was right. The fact that almost all his assistants were foreign had added to the complications.

Cabrini accompanied them outside. Chavez was standing there watching the unloading. When they appeared he turned to study them with a hostile expression on his bearded face.

Cabrini at once went over to him, and with a grim smile, addressed him quickly in the same foreign tongue they'd heard the others use. Carolyn thought it was of middle-European origin but couldn't be sure. At any rate it was unintelligible to her.

Chavez reacted to the words of his employer by giving the two girls another baleful glance. Distrust was mirrored on his ugly face. Then he shrugged and turned away from them to go over and supervise the unloading of the vans.

Cabrini returned to them, his flashlight off and held by his side. The bald man smiled thinly and said, "Chavez resented my reprimand. But you may be sure he will treat you with much more understanding in the future."

"Thank you," Carolyn said.

Beth spoke up in her frank way, "After tonight he needn't worry about us coming back here again."

"But I hope you will," the tall magician insisted. "I wish to be your friend."

"You can mention us to William Kerr," Carolyn said. "He'll vouch for us."

"Poor blind William," the magician said. "What a fine, gentle man he is. Are you familiar with his poetry?"

"I've read some of his poems," Carolyn said.

"Excellent, aren't they?" the magician asked.

"He is talented," Carolyn agreed.

"And his sister, Adele; how devoted to him she is," the magician continued with a sigh. "He is a most fortunate man in spite of his handicap."

"You really don't notice it after a little," Carolyn said.

"True," the magician agreed.

Beth, who had been watching the unloading, now spoke up. "You do have female assistants after all! We wondered!"

The bald magician's thin face showed interest. "But of course! I have several lovely ladies in my show."

Carolyn gazed over in the direction in which Beth had been looking and saw two girls standing near the vans. They wore dark, cape-like maxi-coats which flared out at the bottom. They both were attractive though extremely pale, and they seemed to be staring at nothing in particular as they waited for the unloading to finish. There was something about them, a certain air of the unusual, which gave Carolyn a feeling of uneasiness.

She turned to the magician again. "Are they both European, as well?"

"Yes," he said. "They don't speak English as yet. But most of my people will pick up a smattering of your language during the tour."

"I suppose they'll be bound to," Beth agreed.

Carolyn took another glance in the direction of the girls and was startled to see that they'd vanished. It was almost as if the magician had waved an invisible wand and caused them to disappear.

She couldn't restrain a gasp. "They've gone!"

His stern face showed grim amusement. "Really? They must have gone into the house." But this did not explain how they'd vanished so quickly.

Beth was studying him. She said, "You speak English very well."

The tall, bald man nodded. "During the Second World War, I was in the service of the British Intelligence Department. I learned the language quickly."

"It sounds interesting," Beth said.

"I assure you it was," the bald man said with one of his glacial smiles.

Carolyn suddenly felt an urge to get away from the eerie scene. The bald man in his black outfit still held some fear for her. And she felt Chavez had to be a villainous character. On top of this one had to consider the weird assistants all speaking a foreign tongue. She felt isolated and in danger. She began to think that for once her Uncle Roger's doubts had been well taken. The arrival of Cabrini might be a mixed blessing for Collinsport. She said, "We must go back to Collinwood."

Cabrini asked, "Is it far?"

"Only a few minutes walk," she said.

"Then you will be all right alone," the magician said.

"Of course," Carolyn said. "We'll no doubt meet again."

The bald man nodded. "And, I trust, under happier circumstances."

Beth looked at him grimly. "They couldn't be any worse, could they?"

"Again I must offer my apologies," Cabrini said politely, though the look on his face and in his eyes suggested that he had enjoyed giving them a thorough scare.

They said goodnight and hurried off into the darkness. Carolyn glanced back once to see the spare, black figure watching after them. When they were a good distance back along the road to Collinwood she gave a sigh of relief and felt ready to discuss their experience.

Turning to Beth, she said, "What did you make of all that?"

"Scary."

"It was."

"But I imagine he's a fine magician," Beth said.

"Probably. He's strange enough."

"Did you think him strange?" Beth sounded surprised.

"He makes me shiver to think about him. He's so tall and thin, and then he has that shaven head and that black outfit he wears! He's weird!"

"It's part of his being a magician," Beth suggested.

"Is it? Or is he simply a strange human being?" Carolyn wondered.

"He has charm."

"A frightening kind."

Beth laughed lightly. "I think the skeleton threw you off and you never did get over it."

"It was a stupid prank for him to play on us."

"He explained. He was testing out an illusion. He couldn't resist the opportunity."

"I think he did it deliberately because he has a cruel streak," Carolyn said. "And that Chavez is either mad or a sadist, or both."

"I didn't care for him," Beth agreed.

"And the others. They all seem so strange. Talking in that foreign tongue. I'm sure the villagers won't take to them."

"The villagers don't like anyone new around," Beth said.

"But these people are so different," Carolyn said, glancing at her friend as they walked on toward Collinwood. "Did you see those girls? How silent and pale they were."

"Probably they were tired after their long journey."

"I don't know," Carolyn worried. "There seemed to be something more about them. As if they were in some kind of spell or daze. They had a lost look!"

"Now you're allowing your imagination to run wild," Beth protested.

"I wonder," she mused. "They surely vanished in a hurry after we began to take notice of them."

"That couldn't have meant anything," Beth objected. "They were probably tired and went inside, as Cabrini said."

"But in a twinkling!"

"It was probably longer than you thought," Beth said. "You may as well admit it. You're prejudiced against Cabrini and his troupe."

"I suppose I am."

"I don't feel the same way. I enjoyed the experience."

Carolyn gave her friend a troubled glance. "You really didn't mind the way we were treated?"

"Not really, since we more or less asked for it," Beth said.

"I know one thing," Carolyn sighed. "I won't dare tell Uncle Roger about any of this. He'd be in a rage and want to have Cabrini and company ordered away from here at once."

"Your uncle is too uptight about such things," Beth said.

"I wonder."

And Carolyn went on wondering after they reached Collinwood. The house was quiet, and both Elizabeth and Roger had gone up to their rooms. With David also safely in bed there was no one to question them. Carolyn was relieved. She didn't want to tell the others of their ordeal until she'd decided whether they'd truly been treated badly or not.

Beth, on the other hand, seemed to have no hard feelings over the incident. Carolyn was worried that the strange, bald magician had exerted his charm to win the pretty, dark girl as a follower. She knew of Cabrini's reputation as a hypnotist and wondered if he had started to exert an influence on her friend. It was a possibility which frightened her.

She said goodnight to Beth and went on to her own room. Exhausted, she fell asleep almost the moment her head touched the pillow. But her sleep was filled with a turmoil of macabre dreams. And in all of them the bald, menacing Cabrini played the role of pursuer. She fancied herself running in terror with Cabrini at her heels. She turned fear-stricken eyes to glance over her shoulder and see him coming after her, his lean, black-clad body moving lithely over the ground and his face stern and angry. She awoke once sobbing out her fear to the quiet darkness of her room. She knew it had been a dream, but she was still haunted by the eerie figure of the magician.

In the morning it was gray and foggy. The sunshine of the previous day had vanished. The fog was so thick she could barely see the cliffs, and the bay beyond was completely misted over. It seemed a suitably grim day for her state of mind. By the time she went downstairs her Uncle Roger had left for the family fish packing plant in Collinsport. But his young son David was still at the table, and he at once began to question her.

"Did you and Beth go to Kerrhaven last night?" the boy wanted to know.

She gave him a weary glance. "We walked a little way."

"You saw them unpacking?"

"Yes."

The boy's eyes were wide with excitement. "Did you talk to any of them?"

"They all speak a foreign language," she said. "And you mustn't go over there. They don't want strangers around."

David looked frustrated. "You and Beth went there!"

"We found it embarrassing. We weren't wanted," she warned him.

He became sullen. "You're saying that just to keep me away."

"Why should I want to keep you away from there if there wasn't a reason?" she asked him.

"You always like to do things I can't do because you're more grown-up," David said disconsolately.

"That's not true."

"It is. And I'll go over there if I want to," David said, rising from the table.

Alarmed, she pleaded with him. "David, you mustn't! Not until we know more about these people."

"You're just like father!" David said, his young face showing anger. "You don't want me to have any fun!" And he ran out of the room, leaving her sitting alone at the dining room table.

She felt suddenly dismayed. She would have to confess their excursion to Roger Collins after all and tell him how she felt about Cabrini and his company. It was the only way she could be sure of protecting David, and all of them for that matter. She was certain the newcomers at Kerrhaven meant the shadow of some unknown threat for the area. Beth may have thought her fear was stupid, but she couldn't help it.

Elizabeth came into the dining room and gave her a questioning glance. "What is wrong with David?"

She sighed. "We had an argument."

"About what?"

"He thinks he should be allowed to go over to Kerrhaven and watch the magician and his company at work. I told him he mustn't."

"You sound very definite on that score. Why?"

"Because Beth and I were over there last night," she said. And awkwardly she explained what had happened, ending with, "I'm not sure what kind of people they are. And I don't think it's a proper place for David to go alone."

"I agree about David for various reasons," Elizabeth said. "But I also wonder if you aren't being too critical of these people. Evidently Beth was more favorably impressed by Cabrini than you."

She nodded worriedly. "That bothers me, too. He seemed to exert some strange authority over her."

Elizabeth smiled wanly. "I think you were scared and it has made you unduly suspicious."

"Perhaps," she said, though she was by no means convinced.

Shortly thereafter Beth came down and they had breakfast together. She could tell that Beth's attitude was the same as it had been the previous night. She believed Cabrini to be an interesting, friendly person. Carolyn hoped her friend might be right.

They moved into the living room after breakfast and were seated on a divan by the window talking when Adele Kerr's car came into the driveway. Carolyn at once jumped up and stared out the window at the familiar blue sedan.

"I wonder what Adele is doing here so early in the day," she asked her friend.

Beth was also on her feet now and gazing out the window. A peculiar expression crossed her pretty face as the dark girl said, "She has someone with her."

"So she has!" Carolyn agreed as the car doors opened. With Adele, to her surprise, she saw a tall, spare figure in a black suit emerge from the sedan. "It's Cabrini!"

Beth smiled. "I had an idea he might show up."

"So soon?" Carolyn glanced at her friend in surprise.

Beth nodded with that impish look in her black eyes again. "I seem to be able to read his mind," she said.

Carolyn frowned, wondering if it weren't the other way around and it was Cabrini who was instilling thoughts in the mind of her friend. But since at that moment Elizabeth answered the doorbell, she made no comment. Her mother greeted the newcomers and there were general introductions all around as Cabrini and Adele Kerr came to sit with them in the living room.

The elderly spinster explained, "Cabrini wanted to pay a visit. My brother was to accompany him, but he is laid low with his arthritis again so I said I would come."

Cabrini, in a neat black suit, white shirt and black tie, looked more like an ordinary person than in the costume he'd worn the previous night. He was still unusual enough with his bald head and thin face, but now he smiled at them all in a genial fashion.

"I hope I have not timed the visit too early," he said. "But I am an early riser and I wanted to get some few errands done."

Carolyn's mother returned his smile. "We're glad you came. We've been talking about you."

He gave Carolyn a grimly amused look as he said, "I'm afraid my assistant and I made a dreadful impression on your daughter and Miss Mayberry last night. We feel very badly about it."

"I'm sure you are forgiven," Elizabeth said.

Adele Kerr spoke up with an earnest look on her lined face. "I must say William hasn't quite forgiven Cabrini. He thinks it was unfortunate to scare the girls as he did. And that is one of the reasons he encouraged Cabrini to pay this call as promptly as possible."

"I wish to make amends," Cabrini said suavely. "And let me begin by noting that you have requested my company give a performance here for charity. We will be delighted to perform for you free of charge if you can provide a suitable stage for the performance."

Elizabeth looked extremely pleased. "I thought of the front lawn. We can get chairs from the hall in Collinsport and I'll have our workmen build a stage to your requirements."

"That would be entirely suitable," the magician said. "You can count on me. I would suggest a day in late July. We can discuss the exact details later. I merely wanted to get the initial arrangements made now."

Adele Kerr was pleased. "My brother more or less promised you would do the show," she told the magician. "He'll be very glad to hear you've agreed."

The bald man said, "Most happy to." He paused. "There is one thing. I would like to have some local assistants on stage with me. Merely to give the show local interest."

Carolyn's mother listened attentively. "That would be a good idea."

Cabrini went on smoothly, "I can think of no two young women more fitted to decorate a stage than your daughter and Miss Mayberry."

Elizabeth turned to Carolyn with a pleased smile. "You'll be glad to take part in the show, I'm sure."

Carolyn was flustered. She felt as if a trap were closing on her. She hastily said, "I don't know. I might be too nervous!"

"Nonsense!" Adele Kerr said. "You're one of those young moderns who don't know what nerves mean."

"Still, I'm not sure," Carolyn protested. What she didn't want to say was that she distrusted the bald magician and didn't like the idea of being in his company and working with his people.

Cabrini turned from her to fix his eyes on Beth. As he did so Carolyn couldn't help but feel there was a special light in them, that he was studying her friend in a certain strange fashion.

The magician smiled and asked Beth, "Surely you won't refuse, will you, Miss Mayberry?"

Beth was staring at him and smiling. "I'd like to take part in the show," she said.

Carolyn wasn't surprised at her friend's ready answer. It only bore out what she already knew: Cabrini had somehow gained at least partial control over the girl's mind. Beth was becoming more and more an automaton under the suave magician's guidance.

Rather helplessly, she turned to Beth and said, "Are you sure you want to take the time to do it?"

"Yes. I am," Beth said in a strangely satisfied tone, but her dark eyes were still on Cabrini.

Carolyn was overwhelmed by a feeling of helplessness and dismay. She debated what to do or say next. But in the middle of her thoughts the doorbell rang. She rose at once and went to answer it, thinking in this way to gain time while the others talked on in the dining room.

She slowly opened the door, and there on the fog-shrouded steps stood a familiar figure in an Inverness cape. It was Barnabas Collins!

CHAPTER 3

Carolyn was unable to conceal her surprise at seeing Barnabas. There had been no word of his coming, but then he seldom let them know. Once she had learned of his arrival through meeting his servant, Willie Loomis, walking along the path by the stables. And another time she'd gone by the old house after dark and noted the glow of candlelight from a single window which had lost its shutter. Thus she knew that Barnabas had installed himself in the old house, which had never been wired for electricity.

But there was a second reason for her surprise. This was mid-morning and here was Barnabas standing on the steps. Because of the curse which he'd so long endured, he never appeared in the daylight hours. During the time between dawn and dusk he sank into a sleep of death and rested in an ancient coffin deep in the cellars of the old house. It was the chief task of his servant to guard him during these hours.

She stared at the grave, handsome face of this cousin from England and said, "Barnabas! I can't believe you're here! And during the day!"

He smiled at her. "I had a feeling I might surprise you. It's all right, I'm feeling very well these days."

"Come in!" she said, collecting her confused thoughts. "Don't stand out there in the fog."

"Thank you," he said in his pleasant, actor's voice, and he came inside and began to divest himself of the coat and cape.

They stood in the shadowed hallway with some murmurs of conversation coming to them from the others in the living room. Carolyn took his coat, and giving a nod toward the entrance of the big room on the right told him, "We have some company."

"So I hear," Barnabas said, studying her. "You're growing into a truly beautiful young woman."

Carolyn blushed at the compliment. For as long as she could remember she'd admired Barnabas. And in recent years her admiration had become more like real love. Several times she'd been certain that he reciprocated her feelings. But always there had been the barrier of the curse between them. He had refused to think of her linking herself to his vampire state.

She said, "What does it mean? Your being here at this hour of the day."

He offered her one of his melancholy smiles. "Look in the mirror," he said, indicating the large hall mirror on the wall near them.

She did and gave a tiny gasp. There in the mirror the figures of both herself and Barnabas were plainly revealed. Never before had she seen his reflection in a mirror. "You've been cured!" she cried.

"I've been treated," he corrected her quietly. "I finally gave in to Dr. Julia Hoffman's pleas and have been taking a series of injections at her clinic. She hopes that I may be cured. At least the vampire state has been suspended for a while. I dare not let myself hope for more than that until some time has passed."

"That's wonderful, Barnabas!" she said excitedly.

"At least I can live like any normal human being while the treatments benefit me," the tall man said. "Who is in there in addition to Elizabeth?"

She quickly told him, ending with, "I'm not sure I like this Cabrini or the strong influence he's suddenly exerting over Beth."

Barnabas frowned. "Cabrini, the magician! I've heard of him."

"You would have," she agreed. "I believe he's very well known in Europe."

"Yes," Barnabas said quietly. "Very well known." She thought there might be an insinuation in his tone, but she had no further time to question him. As it was, the others in the living room might well wonder what had detained her this long. She led Barnabas into the adjoining room to meet everyone.

Elizabeth managed to take the unexpected arrival calmly and introduced Barnabas to Adele Kerr, Cabrini and Beth. Barnabas was polite and gracious. When he came to Cabrini he halted before the tall, thin man in a friendly fashion.

Barnabas said, "I'm sure we've met before. Perhaps in London."

The bald man's thin face showed a shadow of uneasiness. "That is quite possible," he said. "I toured England with my company last year and several years before that."

"You don't remember me?" Barnabas asked.

"I'm afraid not. But then, I meet so many people."

"True," Barnabas agreed. "And so you will be here for the summer?"

"Yes. We're getting a new production ready for this country," Cabrini said in his suave fashion.

Adele Kerr spoke up, telling Barnabas, "You must come to the cottage and meet my brother William. I'm sure he'd enjoy knowing you. He is a poet of modest reputation."

"Thank you," Barnabas said to the elderly woman. "I'll be a guest at the old house for some time. I'll be happy to take advantage of your invitation."

Cabrini turned to the spinster and said, "I don't wish to hurry you, Adele, but I have many things to do this morning."

The prim, elderly woman at once rose from her chair. "Of course," she said. "I'd forgotten. We really must be going."

Elizabeth smiled at the two. "You must visit us again soon, and bring your brother, Miss Kerr. And we'll look forward to the performance here on the grounds you've promised us, Cabrini."

He nodded. "You may count on it." He turned to Carolyn and Beth who were standing together. "I hope both you girls will take part in the local presentation." He smiled and fixed his eyes on Beth in particular as he added, "And even if Miss Collins cannot bring herself to join my show I hope you will, Miss Mayberry."

Beth looked pleased. "I look forward to it," she said.

Once again Carolyn was shocked by the way her friend responded to the bald, older man. There seemed little doubt that Cabrini had some macabre talent for influencing people. She recalled her brief glimpse of those two wan-faced girls standing near the trucks the previous night and hoped that Beth would not wind up like them. They had seemed little more than puppets to be manipulated by the master magician.

These were the thoughts going through her mind as her mother saw the two to the door. Now she was alone in the room with Barnabas and Beth. She at once attempted to let them get to know each other better. She explained to Barnabas about Beth's parents being in Japan and told the girl that Barnabas had also traveled in the Far East.

"Did you spend a long time in Japan?" Beth asked him.

"I was there for nearly six months," Barnabas said. "But that was some time ago. I'm sure the country must have changed a good deal since."

Beth said, "It's changed a lot just these last few years. At least that's what my parents have written me. It's becoming very western in its way of living."

"I would expect that," Barnabas said. Then he added, "Cabrini is a strange type, isn't he?"

She said, "He has a mysterious air about him. It frightens me a little. But I suppose it is an asset to him as a professional magician."

Beth's pretty face showed a shadow of annoyance. "I don't find him at all frightening. I think he's very nice."

Barnabas glanced at her. "Have you known him long?"

Beth shook her head. "The first time I saw him was last night."

"I wouldn't try to judge him too quickly. He's the sort of person it takes some time to know. He's bound to be complex and have undertones to his character which you'd never expect from a casual meeting."

Beth looked unimpressed. "I feel I know him well enough."

Carolyn was unhappy with her friend's reply but she wanted to discuss it alone with Barnabas. So later in the day she set out in the fog to seek him at the old house. The heavy mist gave an eerie touch to the grounds. The tall trees were mostly hidden by the fog with only their lower branches visible.

By the time she reached the old house she could not see Collinwood through the fog. She felt lost and isolated in the sea of gray as she mounted the stone steps of the ancient house and knocked on its oaken door.

A moment or two passed before the door was opened a crack and the somewhat stupid face of Willie Loomis peered out at her from the shadows. "Yes?" he said, sulky in this greeting.

"I want to speak with Barnabas," she told him.

He looked uncertain. "I don't know," he said.

"Is he in?"

Willie hesitated. "Yes."

"Then tell him I'm here and he'll see me."

"You'll have to wait," the youth said, and he quickly shut the door in her face. She could hear him retreating down the hall inside.

It was all too apparent that he was still conducting himself in the same way he had when Barnabas had been suffering from the vampire curse. Willie was not quick to accept the change in the handsome Britisher.

Now she heard someone coming to the door and it was Barnabas who opened it for her. "Come in," he invited her. "I'm glad to see you."

"I had to talk to you alone," she explained as she entered the dark hallway of the old house.

He showed interest. "I had the impression something was bothering you when we met earlier at Collinwood."

"You were right."

He led her down the hallway to the living room of the old house which was smaller in size than the one at Collinwood but equally well furnished. Its dark wood-paneled walls held fine paintings of members of the family.

Barnabas saw her safely seated by the fireplace, and then, standing by it, said, "Now tell me your problem."

She looked up at him anxiously. "You must have guessed. It's Beth."

"Your girlfriend."

"Yes. I feel responsible for her since I brought her here. And from the moment she met Cabrini she's been acting in an odd manner."

"Explain," Barnabas said.

"She's entirely won over by him," Carolyn explained. "She seems to see him as some glamorous figure. I'm beginning to fear he's managed to get her under a hypnotic spell. He has the reputation of being a clever hypnotist."

Barnabas was concerned. "I've heard quite a few things about Cabrini," he agreed. "But it may be you're allowing yourself to take this all too seriously. It could just be that Beth has had an attack of stage fever. Many young women are anxious to appear on the stage and will go through any amount of hardship to achieve their goal."

"No," she sighed, "I don't think she's stagestruck. But she surely seems completely taken in by that Cabrini. And I don't like him. In fact I suppose I'm afraid of him. He's so suave and arrogant. I wonder that William Kerr could be his friend and that he'd wish to bring him here."

Barnabas stared down at her in the murky atmosphere of the living room. He said, "You're saying you believe Cabrini is evil?"

"I guess that's it," she admitted.

He surprised her by observing quietly, "It is possible you are right about him."

Her eyes widened. "What do you know of his reputation?"

"Not enough," Barnabas said with a slight frown. "However, I have friends who know him better than I do. I may be able to get some interesting information from them."

"I wish you would," she begged. "And soon. Before Beth becomes too involved with that strange man. I can't even guess his age with his head shaven the way it is. His face is bony but not lined."

"Cabrini is much older than he pretends," was the opinion of the man standing by the fireplace. "He cloaks himself in mystery for more than one reason."

"We must try to save Beth from him. I'm going to refuse to take part in the magic show even though it's to benefit mother's hospital charity. And I hope Beth will also not go in it."

The deep-set eyes of Barnabas were sympathetic. "I don't want to worry you needlessly," he said, "But I have an idea she will insist on taking part in the performance."

"I've been afraid of it. That's why I'm asking you to do something."

"I'll try. I can't promise anything."

"Did you actually meet Cabrini in London, as you said this morning?"

"Yes," Barnabas said. "But I was with other friends. I can believe that he didn't notice me."

"So you do know something of him."

"A little but not enough," Barnabas said. "You must be patient. Give me a few days."

"I have no choice," she said with another sigh. "I'm glad you're back for this crisis. And I'm sure you'll be able to help."

He smiled grimly. "I appreciate your faith. I'll try to deserve it. Among other things I'd like to visit this William Kerr."

"The new owner of Kerrhaven," she said. "Adele, his sister, gave you an invitation this morning."

"I intend to accept it," Barnabas said. "What sort of man is he?"

"Old and stooped and he wears dark glasses because of his blindness," she said. "He's very kind and unsuspecting. I can realize how a person like Cabrini could gain his friendship and make use of it. That poor old man would be no match for the wily evil of a person of that type."

"And Adele is also elderly," Barnabas pointed out. "Though she does seem very sharp in mind."

"She's a nice old woman, but neither she nor her brother are all that worldly-wise," Carolyn worried.

Barnabas gave her a tolerant smile. "And you feel you are?"

She blushed. "I may not be as cynical as Uncle Roger but I'm not easily taken in either."

"I'm certain of that."

She rose with a sigh. "I must get back to Collinwood and change for dinner," she said.

"Suppose I come by early in the evening and you escort me over to the cottage to visit with the Kerrs?"

"I'd be glad to," she said. "And perhaps you can use the visit to warn William Kerr that Cabrini may not be everything he thinks."

Barnabas showed hesitation. "I don't want to be too blunt with my views of our magician friend, especially since my information is still incomplete. But maybe I can put Kerr in the mood to ask a few questions."

"I'll leave it with you," she said. And looking up into the gaunt, handsome face with fond eyes, she added softly, "It's so good to have you back."

"I'm happy to be back. And thanks to Julia Hoffman this is a rather special visit." As he finished saying this he took her in his arms, and she at once was thrilled by the pressure of his warm lips on hers. When they had last kissed those same lips had possessed the coldness of death.

During dinner, back at Collinwood, Roger was thoroughly upset by the news that Elizabeth had arranged with the magician to give a performance on the lawns of Collinwood.

From the head of the dining room table he scowled at her. "I don't remember giving my permission for this affair!"

Elizabeth said, "I mentioned it to you and you made no protest."

"That's right," David told his father. "And I want to see the show."

Roger glared at his son. "This isn't to be a private entertainment just for your benefit. If your Aunt Elizabeth has her way she'll have all the county seated out on our lawn. What kind of shape will it be in afterward?"

"It will do less harm than a bazaar or garden party out there," Carolyn's mother insisted. "And we've had a number of them over the years."

"I don't consider the lawn a suitable place for a theatrical entertainment," Roger objected.

"We'll have a stage erected and the performance will be given at night," Elizabeth said. "I think it should be a memorable occasion."

"I'd expect it to be a disaster."

Carolyn made no contribution to the discussion. She was secretly hoping that Elizabeth would lose her argument, but she saw this wasn't likely. Her mother was going to force Roger to agree to the show. Beth also remained quiet through the talk.

Elizabeth said, "Now that Barnabas has returned he may be willing to help arrange the performance. He's very good at such things."

Roger frowned. "I'm not much happier about the return of our cousin than I am about all those foreigners taking over Kerrhaven."

"Barnabas seems very well," Elizabeth said.

"That remains to be proven," Roger said coldly.

Shortly after dinner the doorbell rang and Carolyn answered it. She was startled to see the squat form of the hunchback, Chavez, standing on the front stoop. The ugly little man in his black soft hat and trenchcoat held out an envelope for her.

"For the Señorita Mayberry," he said in his heavily-accented fashion.

"Thank you," she said, a slight tremor in her voice as she took the proffered envelope.

With an ugly smile he said, "There is something in it for you also." Nodding curtly, the black-bearded man hurried back down the steps and out to the station wagon. In a moment he was driving away.

Carolyn closed the door and went to join Beth in the living room. She gave her friend the envelope and said, "For you. It's from Cabrini."

"Oh?" Beth looked pleased. She at once opened the envelope and read the single sheet message enclosed in it. She gave Carolyn a smile and said, "He wants us to go over to Kerrhaven tomorrow night for a rehearsal."

She shook her head. "I'd rather not be in the show."

"You must," Beth insisted. "Your mother is arranging it."

"I'm still not sure."

"At least attend the first rehearsal with me," Beth said. "Let's see what it's like."

Carolyn put her friend off with an evasive answer. But she guessed that in the end she'd probably attend the rehearsal, if only to keep a watchful eye on the other girl. David called on Beth to play checkers with him and this freed her to go out and keep her rendezvous with Barnabas. Shortly after eight she put on her raincoat and kerchief and went outside to wait for him.

He was not long coming. The sight of him approaching through the heavy mist in his caped coat gave her a feeling of security. She was counting on Barnabas to deal with the problem of Cabrini, and she felt sure he wouldn't let her down.

Coming up to her, he smiled and said, "I'm glad you came out here. It spares me the dubious pleasure of having to meet Cousin Roger."

"I thought you'd rather avoid a talk with him now," she said.

"There'll be plenty of time later," he said. "Let us go on to Kerrhaven. Any new developments with Cabrini?"

As they walked across the lawns to the road that led to the adjoining estate she told him about the letter that had been delivered and that Cabrini had invited them to take part in a rehearsal.

"About what I expected," Barnabas commented. "Now I'm

interested in meeting this Kerr and hearing his views of Cabrini."

It turned out rather different from what they'd expected. William Kerr and his sister greeted them in a friendly enough fashion. But the blind poet had little to say about Cabrini except that he found him a pleasant companion. It struck Carolyn that the wealthy estate owner was being careful to back up his judgment in renting the mansion to the Cabrini troupe. What was surprising was the interest he suddenly showed in Collinwood and its people.

From his easy chair the blind man asked Barnabas, "What do you know about the vampire curse of Angelique?"

"How do you know about that?" Barnabas was surprised.

William Kerr smiled wisely, and leaning forward so that the overhead light cast a glint on his thick head of white hair, he said, "I know more about Collinwood than you guess. I have found its history fascinating. I've had Adele read me everything she could discover on the subject."

"You amaze me," Barnabas said quietly. "I can assure you the curse of Angelique is past history."

"I wonder," the blind man said, the face behind the black glasses strangely placid.

"Why do you say that?" Barnabas asked sharply.

William Kerr spread his hands in a gesture of resignation. "I have heard stories since coming here. Very odd stories. It seems that over the years there have been renewals of the vampire scares that began when your ancestor, Barnabas Collins, was sent away from here."

Carolyn saw the tenseness in the handsome face of her British relative. She said, "A lot of that talk has been ignorant village superstition."

The blind man said, "Perhaps. But you know the old story about smoke and fire. It makes one wonder. I have heard that only a year ago young women of the village were attacked under mysterious circumstances and left with a strange mark on their throats. A mark that could have been made by the fangs of a vampire."

Barnabas frowned. "It would seem some of the village people have been trying to impress you with their exaggerated stories."

Adele Kerr spoke from her chair at the other side of the room. "That is what I have told William. I say there are no such things as ghosts or vampires. I just don't believe in them!"

"My sister is vehement on the subject." The blind man smiled. "How do you feel about it, Mr. Collins?"

Barnabas gave Carolyn a brief worried glance, and then he told William Kerr, "I've already expressed my opinion. I have strong doubts about my ancestor ever having been a vampire. I'm of the opinion the story has been garbled over the years."

"But the fact the legend has persisted and that your ancestor's ghostly presence is said to have been seen in the private Collins burying ground on the nights of the attacks would seem to indicate there is something to be explained."

"Idle gossip around the bar of the Blue Whale Tavern," Barnabas said with a hint of anger.

Carolyn was amazed that the conversation had taken this turn. All her hopes that more might be discovered about the mysterious Cabrini were dashed. Now she had to sit by and listen to Barnabas try to defend the reputation of Collinwood and its people.

"Of course it is true that idle tongues enjoy creating scandal," the blind man agreed. "But when a story is told over a long period of years you wonder. I even hear that you have had difficulty securing domestic help at Collinwood because of the prevalent belief among the villagers that the house is filled with phantoms."

"We have a complete staff, Mr. Kerr," Carolyn pointed out. "So I think you can discount that story."

"Perhaps," he said. "And then I have heard this other monster story. About a werewolf being seen on the estate."

Barnabas said quietly, "It's all part of the same gossip."

"In this case a certain Quentin Collins was mentioned," the blind man said.

"These stories are part of the legends of the area," Barnabas told him. "I wouldn't give them a second thought."

"Exactly what I've told my brother," Adele Kerr said promptly. "Now you must stop talking about these unpleasant matters and let me get you a snack."

So the evening ended on a relatively pleasant note. Yet Carolyn felt their visit had failed in its purpose and she knew Barnabas must be of the same opinion. As they walked back to Collinwood through the fog and darkness he expressed himself on this.

"I didn't expect Kerr to tackle me about the Collinwood legends," he said grimly.

"Nor did I," she said. "But I was proud of the way you handled it."

He sighed. "Thanks to Dr. Julia Hoffman I could do it without any feelings of guilt. I can only pray her treatments continue to keep me in a normal state."

Carolyn took him by the arm, clinging to him gently as they walked. "They must," she said with quiet desperation.

"He's also heard about Quentin," Barnabas went on. "He seems well informed about the dark shadows of Collinwood."

"That's clear," she agreed.

"The way things turned out I couldn't very well get to the

subject of Cabrini," Barnabas said.

"Perhaps it was just as well. We probably would only have offended them, without changing their opinions about the magician."

"Likely. Still, Miss Kerr is very intelligent."

"She is," Carolyn said. "I must try and have a talk with her alone one day."

"It might prove worthwhile," Barnabas agreed. "In the meantime you'll have to protect yourself and Beth against Cabrini and his crowd the best way you can… if there is a need to protect yourself."

"I'm only worried about Beth," she said.

"I'll contact my friends," Barnabas promised. "I should be able to tell you something in a few days. In the meantime I wouldn't worry."

He saw her to the door and kissed her goodnight. She went inside feeling a little less depressed and went straight up to her bedroom. The foghorn was still giving out its monotonous warning from Collinsport Point when she got in bed. She stared up into the darkness for a while, thinking about the evening, and then she gradually slipped into a deep sleep.

Sometime later she awoke. It was still dark, and almost at once she knew she'd been awakened by some intrusive sound. She sat up in bed and listened. Then she heard the sound again. It was the knob of her door being turned gently. Horror crossed her lovely face as she directed her gaze to the door. And in spite of the almost complete darkness she was able to see it gradually open. Standing in the doorway was a ghostly female figure!

CHAPTER 4

The shadowy figure advanced into the bedroom and Carolyn uttered a muffled cry of fear. Then as it neared the foot of her bed she saw that it was Beth in a filmy nightgown, her hands outstretched and her face blank as she stared ahead of her with unseeing eyes. Beth was either in some sort of trance or sleepwalking!

Carolyn swung out of bed and turned on her bedside lamp bathing the room in a soft light. As she did so Beth halted and a startled expression crossed her lovely face. She lowered her hands and glanced around in bewilderment.

"How did I get here?" she asked Carolyn in a hushed voice.

"You've been walking in your sleep. You didn't tell me you had trouble of that sort."

Beth stared at her aghast. "I've never walked in my sleep before!"

"You must be over-tired," she said, not wanting the other girl to panic.

Beth shook her head. "I don't understand it."

"I wouldn't try. Go back to bed. The important thing is to get rest. It's not liable to happen again."

"It shouldn't have happened at all!"

Carolyn eyed her troubled friend with sympathy. "You mustn't feel badly. No one else need know."

The dark girl frowned. "It's as if I had some sort of shameful weakness. I don't know what to say! How to explain!"

"You mustn't think of it again," Carolyn advised. "Do you want me to go back to your room with you?"

"No," Beth said, looking pale and worried. "I can at least trust myself to do that." She gave her a frightened glance. "You don't think I'll do it again, do you?"

"I'm almost sure you won't," Carolyn said. "It's a sign of nerves. Once you are soundly asleep you'll be all right."

"I certainly hope so," Beth said, her brow furrowed. "I seem to have had some awful dream."

"Oh?"

Beth's eyes were full of fear. "I can't quite remember what it was. But I know it terrified me. I think that hunchback, Chavez, was in it. Then the next thing I knew I woke up here."

She touched the girl's arm to comfort her. "Don't try to remember the dream or worry yourself about the sleepwalking. Go back to bed and keep your mind a blank. Sleep will come."

"I will," Beth agreed and she started for the door. She hesitated before going into the hall.

"Thank you for being so understanding."

"Just don't worry about it," Carolyn said.

She stood by the door until her friend vanished down the hall in the direction of her own bedroom. Then she closed her door. As she slipped back into bed she puzzled over all that had happened and everything that Beth had said trying to find the meaning of the intrusion.

It seemed plain to her that Beth was not in a normal state. It could be excitement about the arrival of the magician's show and the fact she was going to take part in it, or it might even be the result of some hypnotic spell cast on her by Cabrini. Carolyn favored the second theory. She believed the sleepwalking and the nightmare had been in some way induced by the weird magician's hypnotic powers. And she worried for Beth's safety. With this thought plaguing her she finally fell asleep.

Next morning was bright and warm again. All sign of the fog had vanished; it was a perfect summer day. Carolyn dressed and went downstairs. She felt good, when she went into the dining room and found her Uncle Roger still lingering over coffee she realized at once he was in an ugly mood.

He glared at her as she entered the room and sat down at the table on his right. He said, "I knew that Cabrini troupe would bring us all a lot of trouble."

"What do you mean?"

"A man was murdered in Bar Harbor last night."

She was shocked. "That's dreadful! But how was the murder related to Cabrini and his company?"

Roger's stern face was set in a frown. "Bar Harbor is near here."

"So?"

"Some of that Cabrini crowd have heard that it's a rich resort town. Undoubtedly one of them went over there and robbed the summer hotel and killed the night watchman. The hotel safe was looted and the watchman found with his throat torn open!"

"His throat torn open!" she echoed.

Roger nodded. "Yes. The night clerk had gone to the kitchen for a midnight snack and left the watchman to stay by the desk. When the clerk returned the safe had been robbed and the night watchman was on the floor with his throat ripped from ear to ear."

Carolyn covered her ears. "I don't need all the details."

Her uncle smiled sarcastically. "You and your mother are so anxious to have Cabrini and these foreigners here I felt you should know all the details."

"But how can you blame Cabrini or any of his people?"

"The crime was committed after they arrived," Roger said, as if this proved everything.

Carolyn studied him with dismay. "That doesn't make them guilty. You shouldn't make such accusations without proof."

"If the police delve into it enough they'll get their proof," her uncle said in his arrogant way. "I hope it's settled soon. Nothing I'd like better than to see that pack of foreigners sent on their way."

"You're being very unfair," she protested.

"I'm being realistic. We've had no crimes of that sort here in ages. It had to be one of that magician's pack."

"Until you know more you'd be wise not to make such accusations," she warned.

Roger got up from the table. "I suppose you'd rather they stayed on at Kerrhaven until we're either robbed or murdered in our beds."

"I don't think those things will happen."

He smiled coldly. "It will be a little late to worry about it afterward. Do you mean to tell me you like this Cabrini fellow?"

This was an awkward question for her to answer, especially in light of her fears for Beth. She shrugged. "I don't think it is important whether we like him or not. He may still be a completely dependable person."

"I doubt that," her uncle said dryly. "I've rarely seen a man with such an aura of evil about him. I don't think Barnabas liked him either. I could sense the repugnance our reformed British cousin felt for Cabrini."

"You may be imagining that."

"I don't think so," Roger said. "Mark my words. If the police don't close in on that crowd there will be other crimes."

"There could be other crimes without Cabrini or his troupe being guilty of them."

"We're the next likely victims," Roger warned her. "If and when anything unpleasant happens just remember that I predicted it." And he stalked out.

Carolyn was left alone at the table to contemplate her uncle's words. She was as concerned about the evil potential of Cabrini as anyone, but she still didn't believe he would be capable of murder. Or would he?

Beth was late coming down and Carolyn wondered if the dark girl might be ill after her sleepwalking. She hoped not. But she made up her mind to stop by her room on the way upstairs if she didn't show herself before then. She made a feeble attempt at breakfast but was too upset to eat.

Her mother came in just as she was pouring herself some coffee. Elizabeth looked weary. She said, "I think I'll join you in a cup."

Carolyn poured the coffee for her mother and said, "I suppose you've been talking with Uncle Roger?"

Her mother nodded and sighed. "Yes," she said, helping herself to cream and a lump of sugar. "What a state he's in! Did he tell you about the murder?"

"Yes. And he was talking wildly about Cabrini or some of the troupe being to blame."

"I know it," her mother said unhappily. "I tried to convince him the murderer could have been anyone but he wouldn't listen."

"Once he gets an idea in his head, that's it," Elizabeth said, after taking a sip of her coffee. "He doesn't want me having the charity performance here and he'll do almost anything to stop it. That includes accusing the Cabrini crowd of a murder which they probably don't know anything about."

"I agree," Carolyn said. "I think it's awful!"

Their discussion was cut short by Beth's arrival. Carolyn was glad to see her friend even though she looked haggard and nervous. She decided not to talk too much about the murder. So she mentioned it briefly and then turned the conversation into other channels. This was not difficult; Beth seemed upset and anything but alert. She was lost in thoughts of her own, deaf to any outside talk.

Almost the moment Beth had some coffee and toast she complained of a bad headache and left them to go back to her room. This added to Carolyn's worries about her friend. But her suspicions were so fantastic she didn't dare mention them to Elizabeth. She felt her mother would at once put her down as another Roger with his wild theories. Only in Barnabas could she confide.

Shortly after she left the breakfast table she walked out to the cliffs and along the path that led to Widows' Hill. She reached the high point of land over the beach and ocean and had been standing there gazing out at the calm water for only a few minutes when she saw Barnabas walking across the field to join her.

The sight of him in his caped coat at once reassured her. She was able to offer him a forlorn smile when he came up to her. She said, "I came out here in the hope of seeing you."

"It's one of my favorite places," he agreed. "You look worried."

"I am," she said. She told him about Beth's sleepwalking the night before and then asked him if he'd heard about the murder.

The tall, handsome Barnabas looked concerned. "Yes. I didn't like the sound of it at all."

"Uncle Roger blames it on Cabrini."

"Why?"

"Apparently he has something against foreigners and magicians," she said resignedly. "Mother believes it is because he resents the idea of our having the show here. He's afraid the grounds will be ruined."

Barnabas looked grimly amused. "Roger has definite ideas and he does have a suspicion of strangers. I won't say the murder wasn't the work of one of the Cabrini troupe but I will point out it could well have been someone else."

"I'm sure it was," she agreed. "Even though I'm afraid of Cabrini."

Barnabas gave her a knowing look. "I understand the watchman's throat was ripped."

"Yes. So gruesome!"

His deep-set eyes met hers. "It reminded me of something else."

"Really?"

"Yes. I'm surprised you haven't thought of it."

Her eyes widened. "Please go on."

"It's the sort of crime that was connected with Quentin when he was here a few years ago."

It gave her a shock. What he said was true. "That farmer in the next county," she recalled somberly. "They found him murdered the same way, and because Quentin was in Collinsport the werewolf legend was revived. It was dreadful! But it turned out to have been the work of a mad dog."

"Yes," Barnabas said quietly. "But mad dogs don't rob safes, do they? This time it had to be a human."

"You don't really think it might be Quentin back?" she asked nervously.

"It made me wonder," Barnabas said. "The circumstances of the crime are unusual. But then again, even if Quentin were here I wouldn't jump to the conclusion that he was guilty. At the most I'd consider him a suspect."

"But he isn't here," she said.

"No," Barnabas said, gazing out at the ocean in a preoccupied manner. "So we have to look for other possible guilty parties. I don't expect the murder and robbery to be solved in a hurry."

"Uncle Roger was right in at least one thing," she admitted. "He said Cabrini's arrival would mean trouble for us, and it has."

Barnabas gave her a penetrating glance. "You're still worried about Cabrini's influence over Beth."

"I have to be."

"Try to conceal your feelings about that," he told her. "It won't do any good at this time to seem panicky."

"But we're supposed to go over to Kerrhaven tonight for some kind of rehearsal and I'm frightened," she said.

"If I were going to be here I'd find an excuse to drop in over there," Barnabas told her. "But I have to go to Bangor on an important errand. I won't be back until the morning."

The news wasn't welcome. Carolyn stared up at him with troubled eyes and said, "I'd better make some excuse and refuse to go."

"If you do Beth is liable to go alone," Barnabas warned her.

"I suppose so."

"And that would be worse than your being along. At least you can offer her some sort of protection," Barnabas said.

"So you believe we should go see what Cabrini wants?"

"Yes," he said. "There seems no alternative."

She looked at the handsome man in the caped coat with earnest eyes. "You've promised to find out what you can about him."

"I will," he assured her. "Just give me time."

"I wish you didn't have to leave and be away tonight," she worried.

"So do I," he said. "But that is part of my delving into Cabrini's past. I have some long distance calls to make that I can't put through from here."

They talked a while longer and then Barnabas saw her back to the front door of Collinwood. He promised to get in touch with her as soon as he returned, and he warned her to be careful when she went to Kerrhaven with Beth. Then he walked away to the old house, leaving her alone to cope with her problems.

The day dragged. David begged her to take him to Kerrhaven and she refused, warning him that Cabrini expected privacy. Beth kept to herself most of the afternoon. And it wasn't until dinner that Carolyn asked her whether she felt well enough to go over to the rehearsal.

Beth did look much better. She at once smiled and said, "I wouldn't dream of missing the chance to be in the benefit show. Of course we'll go to the rehearsal."

"Are you sure you're feeling well enough?"

"I'm much improved from this morning," her friend said. "I'll be fine."

So Carolyn resigned herself to another meeting with Cabrini. She didn't much relish the idea of walking over and back in the dark, so she asked her Uncle Roger for the permission to use one of the cars.

He scowled. "You're planning to drive to Kerrhaven?"

"Yes. I'm not anxious to walk, after that murder."

"I should think you'd have enough sense for that," he snapped. "But I can't imagine why you girls want to go over there."

"We're to try out for the show he's giving here," she explained patiently, though she was sure he'd already been told about it.

Roger looked pained. "That's not settled yet. Your mother hasn't convinced me it's necessary."

"I know she will," Carolyn told him with a small smile.

Her uncle sighed. "That's the trouble here. I seem to be having less and less to say about what goes on. Very well, you can use the car. But only because I don't want you walking out in the darkness unprotected. Not because I approve of you going to Kerrhaven where the murderer probably is."

"Please, don't say such things!"

At dusk she and Beth got in the small sports car Roger used for driving back and forth to the fish packing plant. Carolyn was familiar with the car and always enjoyed driving it. The drive would be short tonight but having the car along gave her some confidence.

On the way over she said to Beth, "You ought to be on your guard with Cabrini. Be careful of looking him directly in the eyes. They say he has hypnotic powers and you never know what he might decide to force you to do."

Beth gave her a reproving look. "I don't believe that kind of talk."

"You know there is such a thing as hypnotism."

"Yes."

"And Cabrini is an expert hypnotist. How can you be sure there's no danger?"

"Because I don't believe him capable of that kind of evil," Beth said with conviction.

Carolyn sighed as she guided the car along the lonely, winding road in the darkness. "I wish I could be as sure."

"You've picked up these nonsensical ideas from your Uncle Roger," Beth said, and she turned to gaze out the side window at the woods through which they were passing.

In a moment they had come into the open lawns of the other estate. Carolyn drove the car to the parking area where the vans and cars belonging to the Cabrini troupe were lined up. She turned off the motor and got out with Beth. It was a warm summer night. Across the asphalt yard some of the workers with the troupe were lined up against a wooden fence talking and laughing among themselves. Their glowing cigarette tips danced as the men gestured.

Carolyn was about to suggest they go directly to the door of the old mansion when she saw a bent figure hurrying toward them through the shadows. As he came nearer she recognized Chavez, the hunchbacked assistant to Cabrini.

He halted before Carolyn with a grin on his ugly face. "Señorita Collins and your good friend, we have been waiting for you. Cabrini has asked me to take you to the barn where the rehearsal is under way."

She looked at the squat man with misgivings. "Is Cabrini there?"

"But of course!" said Chavez, still grinning. "Come along with me."

Carolyn turned to Beth and saw that her face was alight with anticipation. With a sigh she decided to follow the hunchback. He ambled ahead of them toward the barn, glancing back every so often as if to make sure they were still following him. From the entrance the barn looked to be in darkness, but when they went inside they saw that a stage with a backdrop of black curtains had been set up at the far end. The empty stage was lit by several spotlights.

"Where is Cabrini?" she asked the hunchback.

Before he could reply there was a chuckle from beside her. She turned and was shocked to see Cabrini standing there smiling coldly. He was wearing the same sort of black sweater and tights she'd seen him wear that other night.

She said, "You seem to have come out of nowhere!"

Cabrini continued to smile. "In my line of work you have to be adept at swift movements. Surprise is the major element of our effects."

Beth studied the tall, bald man with admiration. "I think you're very clever."

He bowed. "Thank you." While he spoke he let his left hand

briefly touch his right wrist and in a twinkling he was holding a huge bouquet of mixed flowers in his left hand. He offered them to her. "Flowers for a lovely lady," he said.

Beth took the bouquet and held it to her. "It really is magic!" she gasped.

Cabrini looked pleased. "I can perform many more difficult feats," he assured her. He turned to Carolyn and his nimble fingers reached for the kerchief she'd tied around the neck of her blouse. She tried to draw back but in a matter of seconds he had it untied and in his hands.

Smiling at her he held it by two corners between his hands. "A remarkable kerchief," he said.

"It's quite ordinary!" she protested, reaching out for it. "Please give it back to me!"

"In one minute," the magician said with a strange glitter in those hypnotic eyes. "First, let me prove my statement. I said it was a remarkable kerchief and it truly is!"

As he spoke he began taking yards of colored ribbons from the middle of the kerchief. They were of red and yellow and green and there seemed to be no end to them. When he finished producing the ribbons he began drawing out a rainbow series of silk hankies, their ends knotted to form a continuous production. When he'd finished he had his right arm draped with the colorful silks.

Beth clapped her hands in admiration as they stood there in the semi-darkness. Cabrini gave her another of his wise smiles. Then he rolled all the silks and ribbons into a huge ball and raised it up in the air above his head to suddenly vanish!

"I don't believe it!" Beth exclaimed.

"All due to the unusual kerchief," Cabrini said in his suave way as he returned Carolyn's kerchief to her unharmed.

She took it, saying, "Your performance was impressive. I see that you live up to your fine reputation."

"I have dedicated my life to my art," Cabrini said with another bow to her. He had a slight accent and his manner had the stiff formal quality of the Old World.

Carolyn returned the kerchief to her throat and asked, "Just what is it you want us to do?"

Cabrini appeared very relaxed. "All in good time," he said. "Let us walk down to the stage."

As they walked the length of the barn Carolyn decided to try a test on him. She said as casually as she could, "Did you hear about the murder last night?"

They had only gone part way to the stage but he halted and studied her with those burning eyes. "The robbery and killing in Bar Harbor," he said.

"Yes," Carolyn replied. She was struck by his strong reaction to her mention of the crime.

The bald man in the black outfit continued to stare at her strangely. He said, "A most revolting incident. I understand the victim had his throat torn open brutally."

"I wish you wouldn't talk about it all the time, Carolyn," Beth reproached her.

She pretended innocence. "I just wondered if Cabrini had heard about it."

He smiled coldly, the bony face looking more like a skull with his teeth revealed. And he said, "Miss Collins is quite right in bringing the matter up. It concerns all of us here in the area. In fact the police were here to question me about the movements of my people this afternoon."

"Were they?" Carolyn asked, at once interested.

"Yes," the bald man said. "I did all I could to help them. But of course I knew that none of my company could be capable of such a crime. And I'm sure I convinced them of the same thing before they left."

Carolyn asked, "Do they have any other suspects?"

He nodded. "Yes. They believe it was the work of a madman. Some transient who happened along. They claim that over the years there have been several crimes of a similar type in which the victim's throats have been torn open. They think it could be the same insane character returned and they are keeping a close lookout for him."

She felt increasing alarm, becoming certain that he must be referring to Quentin Collins. He no doubt had heard about the werewolf legend from his close friend, William Kerr. The blind man had seemed to be fully informed about all the eerie happenings at Collinwood over the years.

There was a slight tremor in her voice as she asked, "Did they tell you his name?"

The bald man shook his head. "No," he said. "But surely you must have some idea of who it might be. You have grown up here."

He had neatly trapped her but she could still pretend ignorance of what he was talking about. She said, "I'm afraid I'm not well-grounded in the history of Collinsport's crimes."

"Then why harp on them so!" Beth reprimanded her. "Let's get on with the rehearsal and forget that awful murder."

The bald Cabrini gave Beth a smile of encouragement. "I can see that I have an eager disciple in you, my dear. I shall give you a prime spot in the benefit show." And he resumed walking down to the stage with them.

When they were finally standing in front of the stage he clapped his hands twice in an authoritative manner. The curtains at the rear of the stage parted and the two young women whom Carolyn had seen on her first visit to Kerrhaven came forward wheeling a seven-foot high apparatus between them. They were dressed in blue denim slacks and modish blue sweaters. Neither of them showed any expression; as soon as they had placed the piece of equipment in the middle of the stage they turned and vanished wordlessly through the rear curtain.

Cabrini gave Carolyn a confident glance. "You will notice that my assistants have also been expertly trained."

"They seem to be puppets obeying your commands," she said.

He nodded. "Their minds are carefully attuned to my wishes," he agreed. "Now if you will come up on the stage with me I should like to introduce you to the illusion you will be used in."

She allowed him to take her by the arm and lead her up the several steps to the stage. Once there she saw that the apparatus was a sort of guillotine with a huge steel blade operated by a lever. Below it was a circular opening slightly larger in size than a human head.

Cabrini smiled at her and, working the lever, caused the blade of the guillotine to drop several times. It came full force on a wood block at the base of the opening. She could see that it marked the hard wood each time.

The bald man in black assured her, "The blade is extremely sharp. Let me prove it to you." He bent down quickly and retrieved a huge turnip which had been stored on the base of the machine. "A turnip whole and complete," he said suavely. Then he placed it on the wooden block in the circular opening and manipulated the lever. The blade came crashing down and Carolyn saw the turnip split neatly in half.

Cabrini looked at her with cold amusement. "I warned you the blade was sharp," he said. And he used the lever to lift the blade as he cleared away the sections of the turnip.

As he finished he glanced at her again, but this time there was more than amusement in those deep-set eyes. They glittered with sheer hatred. She felt a cold chill as he stared at her. Then with no warning at all he abruptly seized her and in a second had her on her knees before the guillotine, her head through the opening. She was too shocked to struggle until that instant, but by then it was too late. She heard him jerk the lever and felt the deadly blade drop down to decapitate her!

CHAPTER 5

She screamed. Her eyes closed tight, she heard the blade rattling down. The moment passed; she was still alive, limp and perspiring but surely alive. She looked up and saw the bald Cabrini standing by the guillotine smiling down in his arrogant way.

"It's true," he assured her in his easy fashion. "You're not hurt."

"It was a cruel trick!" she cried, as he helped her up from her knees.

"You must forgive me," the magician said. "It was the best way to let you understand the full effect of the illusion. I wanted you to experience it as the audience will. And Beth as well."

From the front of the stage Beth exclaimed. "It was terrifying and marvelous. I expected Carolyn's head to topple off on the floor."

"Which is exactly what I wanted," Cabrini said. He indicated the lever of the guillotine blade. "There is a special catch on the lever. When I use it the blade is not really released. It just seems to be."

She was shocked and angry. "You might have told me!"

Cabrini spread his hands. "And ruin the effect? That would have been stupid."

"I thought you meant to kill me!"

He smiled. "You should have known better than that. This is the illusion in which you'll appear. And you need never have any more fear since you know it is perfectly safe."

Still annoyed, Carolyn said, "I'm making no promises I'll be in the show."

"But your mother is counting on you," Cabrini said. "And so am I. Now it is Miss Mayberry's turn."

"What do I do?" Beth asked anxiously.

Cabrini smiled. "You shall see." And he clapped his hands twice. The two girls came out onto the stage again and rolled back the guillotine. When it was removed they brought out a coffin and set it up on its end in the middle of the stage. Without even glancing at Carolyn or the magician they vanished once again.

Cabrini spoke to Carolyn. "I'll not need you any longer. I'd like you to watch this illusion from the body of the barn. Don't stand too close to the stage or the effect will be ruined."

She said, "I hope you're not going to scare Beth as you did me."

"No need to worry about that," he assured her.

She left the bald man on the stage and went down the several steps to join Beth in the darkness. Beth merely smiled at her and hurried on up to take her place with Cabrini. Carolyn moved back a distance from the stage wondering what the magician had in mind.

"We will dim the stage lighting," the bald man in black said. "We must have subdued lighting for an attempt to reach out to the spirit world."

As the lights dimmed Beth asked, "What now?"

The bald man gave her a penetrating glance and took her by her right hand. "You will stand in the coffin facing the audience," he told her.

Beth hesitated. "Coffins frighten me," she said.

Cabrini laughed softly. "You need have no fear of this one. Just step inside it." And he guided her into the upright, open coffin. Beth stood there looking embarrassed.

Staring up at the stage with its dim blue lighting Carolyn began to feel uneasy for her friend. Though her own fear had barely left her, she was afraid that something horrible might happen to Beth.

Cabrini moved to the left side of the stage and all at once an eerie musical background began. It had a strange, wailing, Eastern quality which upset Carolyn further. The dim blue lighting seemed to fade until she could barely see the figures on the stage. Now Cabrini came to stand slightly to the left of the coffin in which Beth waited.

The magician made a few passes with his hands and murmured something which Carolyn could not make out because of the weird music. As she watched, a startling thing began to happen on the stage. The standing figure of Beth in the coffin began to slowly fade and in her place a skeleton began to form. Carolyn gave a small cry of fear as she witnessed the transformation. Finally there was only the skeleton in the coffin!

Cabrini clapped his hands once and the skeleton vanished, leaving the upright coffin empty. Then he clapped a second time and the stage lights came up fully bright.

A look of triumph on his face, he addressed Carolyn. "What did you think of that?"

"Where is Beth?" she demanded, moving toward him quickly.

Cabrini smiled. "She is safe. The important thing is that I changed her into a skeleton and made her disappear before your eyes."

"I know it was a trick," she said, "but where is she now?"

"Backstage," Cabrini said. "The illusion is worked out with plate glass reflections, lights and curtains. The timing must be perfect."

"I'm convinced of your talents," she said curtly. "I'm asking to see Beth."

The bald man looked amused. "You still don't trust me, do you?"

"Is that important to you?" she asked.

"Not really," the magician said, his odd burning eyes fixed on her. "But I think it would be more comfortable for both of us if we could be friends."

"Our friendship depends on you and your actions," Carolyn told him.

"I see," he said. And he left her to go to the rear black curtain. He pulled it aside to form an opening, there Beth appeared and joined him on the stage. The moment Carolyn saw the dark girl she thought there was something different about her. She had the same blank look on her face as the other two female assistants.

Carolyn quickly mounted the stage and went to her. "Are you all right?" she asked.

"Yes. Why do you ask?"

"You seem in a strange mood," she said.

"No," the girl said. "I'm perfectly all right."

Cabrini smiled at Carolyn. "Your fears were for nothing, Miss Collins. I'm not the ogre you try to make me."

"That's comforting," she said. "Do you need us any longer?"

"No," the magician said. "Not tonight. But we will need other rehearsals before the performance. I will let you know."

"Then we can leave now?"

"Yes, of course. I'll walk with you to your car. One cannot be too careful these nights after what has happened."

Carolyn had an idea he was mocking her by pretending to be so concerned about their safety. Yet she could not be sure. Cabrini was certainly a complex character. She noticed that it was Beth's arm he took and Beth to whom he addressed his conversation as they walked from the barn to the outside night and the car. He stood by as they got in the car and waved as they drove away.

Carolyn waited a moment before she turned from the wheel to look briefly at her friend and say. "That was an odd experience, wasn't it?"

The pretty dark girl was staring straight ahead as if preoccupied with her thoughts. "I found it pleasant," she said.

"What happened when you went backstage?"

"I just stood there and waited."

Carolyn frowned as she studied the road ahead under the glare of the headlights. "Didn't you see the other two girl assistants?"

"No," Beth said in the same aloof fashion.

Carolyn wasn't satisfied with her friend's responses. She gave her another quick glance. "But they must have been backstage with you!"

"It was all shadowed. I don't know."

"You're sure you're feeling yourself? Cabrini didn't put you under a hypnotic spell, did he?"

"No." But there was a false ring to the denial.

"You're not talking to me the way you usually do," she said. "Are you angry with me or is your mind confused?"

"Neither."

"There must be something wrong," Carolyn insisted.

"I'm tired. I want to get some sleep."

"We'll be at Collinwood in a few minutes," she assured her friend as she turned the car into the private road that led to the old mansion. "Do you still want to be in the show?"

"Yes," the girl said. "I'd like to join Cabrini's troupe as a regular member."

Carolyn brought the car to a halt in the Collinwood parking area. She gazed at Beth in consternation. "You must be joking! You can't mean that!"

"I do," Beth said solemnly. "I'm sure I'd like the life."

"Cabrini must have hypnotized you to make you think things like that," Carolyn exclaimed.

Beth looked at her rather blankly. "No," she said, still appearing dazed. "I'm sick of my dull existence. I think Cabrini is the most interesting man I've ever met."

With that the pretty dark girl let herself out of the car and began walking toward the house. Carolyn followed her, not knowing what to think. Beth was continually becoming more aloof and confused. She tried to catch up to her, but by the time she reached the entrance hall the other girl was well on her way upstairs. Carolyn stood at the bottom of the stairway and watched her with troubled eyes.

"How did you make out?" Elizabeth asked, coming out of the living room.

She turned to face her mother and said, "I can't really tell you. I had a miserable evening. But Beth seemed to enjoy the experience."

Elizabeth glanced toward the stairs. "I was going to question her but she seemed in a hurry."

Carolyn grimaced. "There's something strange about her. I don't understand it."

Her mother asked, "Did Cabrini rehearse you in some of the show's numbers?"

"Yes."

"Well, that is why you went over there," her mother said. "I'm hoping we can stage the show here next week. I'm going to talk to William Kerr about it tomorrow."

Carolyn gave her mother a troubled look. "I'd rather not be in the performance," she said.

"But you must. Cabrini has been kind enough to offer his services for free. And Beth is willing to help."

"I'm sure he's hypnotized her. She's not able to think straight any longer."

Her mother was surprised. "Now you're being as ridiculous as your Uncle Roger. Why should Cabrini hypnotize Beth?"

"To gain control of her. He has two girls in his company now who act weirdly. They seem to be lifeless unless he gives them a command. Now Beth is slipping into that same condition."

"You're letting your imagination run away with you," Elizabeth protested. "Why should Cabrini do such a thing?"

"I don't know yet," Carolyn said unhappily. "But I think my fears are justified."

"And I think you've been listening too much to your Uncle Roger. He sees villains and bogeys in every foreigner. And of course Cabrini and his company have really sent him into fits. You mustn't take on his viewpoint."

"What I feel has nothing to do with him."

Her mother sighed. "You may think not, but I'm sure it has." And with that she too went upstairs leaving Carolyn alone in the shadowed foyer.

She moved across the hall to stare up at the painting of Barnabas which had hung there as long as she could remember. It seemed he was the only person she could turn to. She could only hope the effect of Dr. Hoffman's cure would last. When Barnabas returned in the morning she would tell him the latest development at Kerrhaven.

With a sigh she turned from the painting and went over to make sure the front door was locked. Then she looked out the window beside the door. It was a dark night but there was no fog. As she stared into the shadows she thought she saw a figure moving across the lawn.

Rigid with fear she strained to see in the darkness and recognize the bent, squat shape. It was Chavez, Cabrini's hunchback, shuffling toward the other side of the old mansion. When he was almost opposite her location he paused to glance up at the windows in the upper part of the house. Now she could clearly see his ugly features above the black beard. After a moment he resumed walking and vanished in the shadows.

Her heart was pounding as she drew back from the window. What was Chavez doing on the grounds at this late hour? Was he spying on them for some evil purpose? Scouting the estate for Cabrini? There had to be some motive for his being out there.

Troubled in mind she ascended the stairs and went to her own bedroom. She debated whether to try Beth's door and then decided it would be best not to disturb her friend. There was little chance of Chavez getting into the house, so it seemed best not to bother her.

Carolyn quickly undressed and got into bed. She fell asleep almost at once. But then the nightmares came. She stirred and moaned in a restless sleep as Cabrini threatened her in this fantasy world. She was on the stage again and imprisoned on the block of the guillotine. A mocking Cabrini stood by her with his hand on the lever. She screamed for help but no one heard her. Then Cabrini let the heavy steel blade crash down on her neck. Though her head was severed from her body and rolled helplessly across the floor of the stage she did not lose consciousness.

She was able to think clearly and knew she was a prisoner in her severed head. She saw a shadow swoop down. Cabrini picked up her head in his hands. With an evil smile on his face he told her he was going to mount her head on a pedestal and have her answer questions as a freak attraction for his show. She cried out her fear and hatred of him as he lifted her head high and threatened to hurl it into the darkness. She shrieked out an appeal for mercy!

Awakened by her own scream, she sat up in bed and stared into the shadows of the room. As she became aware of her surroundings she discovered new terror not of the nightmare variety. Someone was standing at the foot of her bed gazing at her.

"No!" she cried hysterically.

The figure moved quickly to her bedside. "It's all right," a male voice said. And in the next instant the lamp on her bedside table was snapped on and she saw the face and form of Quentin Collins!

"Quentin!" she gasped.

The good-looking young man with the heavy sideburns smiled as he touched a finger to his lips. "Not so loud," he said. "I'm not ready to announce myself to the whole house yet."

She stared at him, not yet believing he was real. "What are you doing here?"

The young man said, "If you mean why am I here in your room, it's because you screamed out. You screamed so loudly I was sure you were in some sort of trouble, so I came into you."

"I had a nightmare," she confessed. "A dreadful nightmare!"

"It must have been dreadful to make you scream like that," Quentin said.

"But how did you come to be in the house in the first place?"

Quentin's eyes twinkled. "I have come to pay a visit. I arrived late so I used a key I still own to come in by a side door."

"None of the others know you're here?"

"Not yet, unless your scream roused them and they come here." He glanced toward the closed door to the hall. "There's no hint of them yet so I'd say we're still safe."

She shook her head worriedly. "You've come at a bad time."

"Oh?"

"There was a murder in Bar Harbor. The victim had his throat ripped open. The police have been everywhere asking questions."

The good-looking Quentin gave a low whistle and sat on her bedside. "Tell me more."

She looked at him uncertainly. "Do I have to? Because of the kind of killing it was your name was brought up. Uncle Roger was relieved that you weren't in the area."

"Did he believe I might be the killer?"

"He at least felt you might be blamed," she said. "There was that other time."

The young man with the sideburns looked grim. "I remember too well," he said. "The local police were ready to take me in custody on the basis of that ancient werewolf legend. You'd think in this day and age you could at least count on the State Police not to believe in Black Magic."

"Superstition dies hard," she said.

"I've learned that," Quentin said grimly. "Even when a mad dog was proven the killer, people still looked at me suspiciously."

"The villagers still think you turn into a werewolf at certain times of the moon," Carolyn reminded him.

He nodded. "If it's not a werewolf they're frightened of it's a vampire. Where is Barnabas these days?"

"He's here at the old house," she said. "At least he was. He went to Bangor on some business overnight."

Quentin gave her a meaningful look. "The kind of business that has to do with young women's throats?"

She shook her head. "No, Quentin! You mustn't think that. He's cured. At least temporarily. He came here directly from Dr. Julia Hoffman's clinic and he's normal. He even hopes the cure may last."

"I've known him to hope that before," Quentin said in a wry voice.

"But this time it's different," she protested. "Dr. Hoffman used the latest scientific treatments to help him. She's done wonders."

There was a mocking light in Quentin's eyes. "I guess you are aware that Julia Hoffman is in love with Barnabas. That's why she's so anxious to cure him."

"I know she likes him. I've always felt they were just good friends."

Quentin smiled. "She's in love with him. But then so are you. Don't bother to deny it."

She blushed. "This is no time to discuss that."

Quentin stood up beside her bed. "You're right. I must find myself a bed and get some sleep. If I'm found wandering around in the darkness they'll surely want to tag me a werewolf."

Carolyn stared up at him anxiously. "It's no joke, Quentin!"

"I know that," he said in a sober voice.

"I realize you have your problems just as Barnabas had," she went on. "But I've never felt you could murder anyone in cold blood."

"Excellent. A vote of confidence."

"Don't make fun of me, Quentin," she begged. "I think you should get away from here at once. If you remain you're bound to be suspected of the murder and all the werewolf talk will be raised again."

"I never run from trouble."

"It's the sensible thing to do. Uncle Roger will be furious if he finds you here in the morning."

"Then he will surely be furious," Quentin said. "I intend to stay. If someone has been committing murders for which I'm being suspected I prefer to remain here and find out something about it."

"I think I know who is guilty," she said.

"Who?"

"A dreadful man called Cabrini," she said. "He's a magician."

"It gets more interesting all the time," Quentin said. "Now I'm sure I'm going to remain."

"He's a vicious man," Carolyn told him. And she quickly explained about her friend Beth, and about her suspicions that the girl was under the magician's hypnotic influence.

Quentin listened and then said, "If he's capable of making people his slaves then he's capable of anything. He's probably behind the Bar Harbor murder in some way. It shouldn't be too hard to find out."

She sank back against the pillows with a deep sigh. "Then in spite of all I've said you still intend to stay here."

"I do, little cousin," Quentin said pleasantly. And he bent forward and touched his lips to her forehead in a tender kiss. "So go back to sleep and don't have any more of those nightmares."

"I'll try not to," she said. "Now I have this extra worry about you."

He smiled. "Don't let me bother your sleep. I always manage

very well. I'll see you in the morning. Shall I turn out the light before I go?"

"No," she said. "Let me do it later."

"Very well," he said. And he moved across to the door. He turned before he went out to say a final, low, "Good night."

When she was alone in the room again she tried to get it all straight in her mind. The arrival of Quentin was an unexpected development and might make everything more complicated. On the other hand she knew him to be clever and resourceful and he might help in getting things straight. She could only hope so.

Barnabas would have something to say about it all. And she generally went by his opinion. The hours until morning would not be too long and then she'd be able to talk with Barnabas and hear what he thought. With this settled in her mind she reached wearily for the lamp switch and turned it out. She lay awake for a long while before sleep came.

The next morning was gray. Dark clouds over the bay threatened rain. But there was no fog. Carolyn dressed quickly to get downstairs and discover how Quentin was being received by the others. She hoped they wouldn't be too hard on him.

As she started down the final flight of stairs she heard angry voices and saw Quentin and Roger facing each other in the entrance hall. Roger had his hat on, apparently ready to leave for his office in the village, and he was clearly in one of his rages.

"You are deliberately planning to stay here to cause us all embarrassment and worse," he exclaimed.

"I'm surprised at your tone, Roger," Quentin said pleasantly. "You are my cousin and this is the family estate. Why shouldn't I be welcome here?"

"You know very well why," Roger said, his stern face a violent shade of purple. "Even if you weren't responsible for that killing in Bar Harbor there'll be plenty of the local people who'll think you know something about it."

"That's why I plan to stay here," Quentin said. "I'd like to try solving the murder. If what you say is true I'll have to do it to clear my name."

"The reputation of all the family is involved," Roger said. "All I ask is that you get decently away from here before anyone local sees you."

"Too late for that," Quentin said genially. "I stopped by the Blue Whale for a few drinks on my way here last night. I had an idea some of the villagers were looking at me askance and murmuring about me behind my back but I was quite innocent. I had no knowledge of the murder then."

Roger glared at him. "You must be pleased with yourself. You and Barnabas are the renegades of our family. Everytime you return you risk disgrace for us."

Quentin gave him one of his charming smiles. "But then you must admit we are the two most interesting members of the Collins clan, aren't we?"

Roger snorted angrily. "There's no use trying to reason with you!" And he went out, slamming the front door after him.

Carolyn paused on the lowest step and gave Quentin a reproachful smile. "You enjoy taunting him," she said.

Quentin nodded. "He makes such a delightful victim."

"Most of what he said is true."

"I can't agree. I must stay here and try to find the real murderer."

"That's a job better left to the police."

"Except that the police rarely seem to solve these unusual crimes," Quentin said. "I'm going to take a close look at your magician friend Cabrini. What you told me about him last night made me interested."

"He could have nothing to do with the murder."

"I know that," Quentin said. "But one has to begin somewhere. I suggest the next thing we do is have breakfast together."

And they did. It wasn't until they were lingering over coffee that she began to worry about Beth not having put in an appearance. She recalled having seen Chavez last evening. She got up from the table quickly. "I'm going up to see if Beth is all right," she told Quentin.

He stared at her. "You're really upset."

"I'm afraid I am. She should be down here by this time unless she's ill. And she didn't seem herself last night."

"Better go see then," he advised.

She hastily left the dining room, and when she reached the hall she met her mother and asked her if she'd seen Beth. Elizabeth shook her head. "No. Of course you know Quentin has returned. And at the worst possible time."

"I've had breakfast with him," Carolyn said, starting upstairs. "I'm more worried about Beth."

She went straight to Beth's room and knocked on the door. There was no reply from inside. Becoming more nervous she knocked again and waited. When there was no answer this time she tried the door. It opened easily and she went inside. The first thing she saw was that Beth's bed had not been slept in.

Then she saw the neatly addressed envelope on the dresser and picked it up. It was addressed to her. She opened it and read the short note from Beth. It said: "Cabrini has asked me to join his company as a full time member and I've decided to do it. Please try to understand, Beth."

CHAPTER 6

Stunned by the note, Carolyn glanced around the room and saw that Beth had taken her clothing with her. Her suitcases were gone and the single closet was empty. Now the mission of Chavez began to make sense. Beth must have agreed to join Cabrini when she was over at Kerrhaven for the rehearsal. He had sent his assistant to meet her and help her back with her things.

So it had happened! And sooner than she'd expected. She left the bedroom and went downstairs. Quentin had gone out somewhere, but her mother was still there. She showed the note to her.

With a pained expression Elizabeth read the note. Then she looked at Carolyn. "Why would she do such a thing?" she asked.

"Cabrini either talked her into it or hypnotized her."

"I'm sure she must have decided this of her own free will," Elizabeth said.

"I'm not."

"You and Roger are so anxious to make Cabrini seem a villain," her mother sighed. "And I know you're both wrong. William and Adele Kerr wouldn't rent their place to anyone they weren't sure about."

"Cabrini may have been too crafty for them as well."

"No. I don't think so," Elizabeth said. "Beth is just a stage-struck girl. She'll soon find there's little glamor in backstage life, and then she'll be glad to leave Cabrini's troupe."

"I hope so."

"I'm sure of it," her mother said. "She's of age and we are only friends to her. There's really nothing we can do about it."

"I'll send an airmail letter to her parents," Carolyn decided.

"I guess you should do that," her mother agreed. "I hope we have no upset to spoil the show we've planned for here."

Carolyn reproached her. "I believe you are more worried about the success of that entertainment than you are about Beth's welfare."

Her mother looked embarrassed. "You know that's not true."

"I'm not so sure," Carolyn said. She went on into the library and sat at the desk to write a letter to Beth's parents. She explained what had taken place and urged them to write Beth at once in care of either herself or Kerrhaven. She looked up the address and did the envelope. Then she stamped the letter and took it outside to the mailbox.

This done, she decided to walk back to the old house and see if she could find Barnabas. The day was still grim. Dark clouds mirrored her mood. Things were not working out well at all.

When she reached the old house she saw Willie Loomis getting some things from the trunk of Barnabas' station wagon. He looked up when he noticed her.

She asked him, "Where is Barnabas?"

"Inside," Willie said.

"Is he busy?"

"I wouldn't know."

"I'd like to see him for a moment," she said. "Will you tell him I'm here?"

Willie nodded rather sullenly and went inside. After a moment the door opened and Barnabas came out. The sight of the handsome man in his Inverness cape always gave her new hope. He said, "I was on the point of going over to Collinwood to find you."

"Then I've saved you the trip."

"Do you want to go inside?" he asked.

"No. I'd just as soon walk and talk in the open. I don't think it will storm for a while."

"Very well," Barnabas said. "Let's go this way. We won't attract so much attention." And he began walking away from the old house down the sloping field that led to the ancient family cemetery.

"A good idea," she said. "Before I hear your news let me tell you that Beth has left Collinwood to live at Kerrhaven and be a regular member of Cabrini's company."

"That happened suddenly!"

"I know. She left last night. Probably some time after midnight. There was a note for me in her room."

"Did she give any reason?"

"None except that she was sick of living a dull life. I'm sure Cabrini has hypnotized her. She's done this under his influence."

"It could be," Barnabas agreed.

"And my second piece of news is that Quentin is back."

"Quentin!" Barnabas exclaimed as they walked on toward the cemetery.

"Yes. And you know the trouble that can mean. Roger almost demanded that he leave, but he refused to go."

"Does he know about that murder at Bar Harbor?"

"Yes. And about his name being brought up as a suspect. It annoyed him and he decided he'd remain here and see if he can't find the murderer."

"That's not likely."

"I agree. But he intends to stay. So you see everything is in a mess."

Barnabas gave her a wry look. "It begins to seem all your fears about Cabrini were well-founded."

"I despise him!" she said. "And mother is willing to tolerate him because he's offered to do her charity show."

"The success of the hospital fund means a lot to Elizabeth."

"But she shouldn't let it close her eyes to everything else," Carolyn grumbled. "What can we do to save Beth from that man?"

"Not much," Barnabas said.

"It wouldn't do any good for me to go over there and plead with her," she said. "She behaves as if she were in a drugged state."

"Which could be explained by hypnosis."

"It's no use talking to Cabrini. So there are only the Kerrs."

Barnabas nodded. "Yes. And the last time we went over there to approach them the old man began a long-winded harangue about the phantoms of Collinwood."

"We got nowhere," she lamented.

"My being there seemed to make it awkward," Barnabas said. "I feel you would do better if you went to see the Kerrs on your own."

She gave the tall, handsome man at her side an interested look. "It is worth a try."

"I'm sure of it."

"If William Kerr knew the sort of man Cabrini really is I know he'd order him away from Kerrhaven."

"Then you must do your best to influence him," Barnabas said.

When they reached the cemetery gates they went inside the iron fence and moved among rows of headstones, green mounds and occasional tombs. There was a distant rumble of thunder and Carolyn thought she felt a drop of rain on her cheek.

"The storm may be closer than we guessed," she said.

Barnabas glanced up at the cloudy sky. The morning had taken on a look of nightfall. Then the thunder came again, more loudly, and there was a brief show of forked lightning.

"It's getting worse," she said, instinctively pressing close to him.

"We'll need shelter," Barnabas said. "Let's hurry!" And he led her along a path between dozens of graves of long-ago members of the Collins family. At last they came to a large tomb with the name Josiah Collins carved on its front in big letters. The tomb had a rusty iron door and Barnabas opened it without hesitation to reveal the shadowed doorway and the tomb beyond.

"Go on in," he urged her.

The rain had begun to pour down so she didn't hesitate in entering the musty interior of the tomb. Barnabas followed her. It was a few steps below the level of the ground outside. Now they stood close together in the eerie shadows of the tomb as it stormed beyond the partly-open door.

"I didn't think of doing this," she said.

He gave her a wry look. "Enter the world of the dead? I'm more used to it than you."

She looked around the tomb with the rows of coffins stacked on either side of it. "It's all so strange," she said with a tiny shudder.

"I have no fear of these places," he said. "I am no stranger to coffins."

"Please, Barnabas, don't talk like that when we're in here," she begged him. "I'm frightened enough as it is. I don't want to be reminded of what you were."

It was almost dark outside and the lightning cut through the gloom like a sharp weapon. The thunder clamored and the rain came down in sheets. Barnabas had a sober expression on his gaunt face. "And what I could be again."

"You won't revert," she said. "You mustn't."

"It has happened before," he reminded her.

"But you had more modern treatment this time."

A lightning flash allowed her to see his bitter expression. He said, "Modern treatment for an ancient malady."

"I've never seen you so well," she insisted.

"And I have never been so well," he agreed. "But I cannot be sure how long it will last. I have memories of those years of wandering. Those centuries when I was one of the living dead. When I slept each day in my coffin cloaked in cobwebs."

"But you rose above your vampire state," she said. "And now you have really conquered it."

The thunder and lightning came again. In the brief silence that followed, broken only by the torrential rain, he looked at the caskets around them covered with dust. He spoke solemnly. "I knew all the people buried here. The crumpled bones and dust in those coffins were once my friends and neighbors. I walked the earth as their contemporary and saw them and generations like them die to rot in their graves."

"No, Barnabas! Please, stop!"

His expression changed to one of sympathy. "I didn't mean to frighten you. But there are times I feel you don't know what I am. The things I have experienced, the long journey I've made."

"I'd rather not think about it," she said. "I like you as you are now."

The storm continued, and when there was another lull he said, "I have some information on this Cabrini."

"Tell me."

"He is known to the London police authorities. When he was in England Scotland Yard was warned by the French police to watch him closely. He has been suspected of smuggling and other offences. I'll have more details for you later. But at least we know he has a police record."

"I wish I could have told Beth that before he got his hold on her," Carolyn worried.

"You can still tell her."

"She won't listen to me now."

"You can tell William Kerr and his sister. Maybe they'll believe you," Barnabas suggested.

"I can try," she said. "What about Quentin?"

Barnabas shrugged. "He'll have to take care of himself."

"You don't think he killed that night watchman at Bar Harbor?"

"There was a robbery involved as well," Barnabas said. "I have never known Quentin to commit a robbery."

"I thought of that myself," she said. "So he must be innocent."

"We can hope so."

"He is closer to you than anyone else," Carolyn pointed out. "You'll have to help him if you can."

"We'll see, but I can't promise anything."

"I know you will," she insisted.

He gave her an enquiring smile. "Are you in love with Quentin?"

She was startled by his question. "No," she said. "He believes I'm in love with you."

"You sound very interested in what happens to him."

"I don't want him to suffer unjustly for somebody else's crime," she said. "And he has wandered through long years like you, long lonely years under that horrible curse."

"We haven't always been on the same side," Barnabas reminded her.

"But you should have been," she argued. "For I really believe in spite of your many differences you are both much alike."

"I'm not so sure of that," Barnabas said grimly. Then he leaned forward and opened the tomb door all the way. "It's stopped storming," he told her. "At least there are only a few drops of rain falling. No need to stay in this place any longer."

He helped her up the moss-covered granite steps and when they were in the open closed the iron door on the tomb again. With relief she drew a breath of fresh air. It was as if she'd returned to the world of the living once more.

She said, "It's much brighter. I'm sure the storm is over."

"I think so," Barnabas agreed. "I'll take you back." They left the isolated cemetery and walked up the sloping field to the old house. When they reached it he halted and told her, "I have things to do. I'll leave you here and be in touch with you later."

"Will you visit Collinwood tonight?"

"I'm not sure. But I will call soon," he promised. "And I hope when we meet again I'll have all the information we require on Cabrini."

"I hope so," she sighed.

Barnabas gave her a melancholy smile. "You mustn't worry so or you'll spoil your good looks. I wouldn't like that." He took her in his arms and kissed her before they parted.

The rest of the day was uneventful. In the evening Carolyn took the car and drove to the cottage in which the Kerrs were living. She had phoned in advance, and Adele Kerr had urged her to pay the visit. Carolyn drove the car past the barn and main mansion without slowing down. She had no wish to see Cabrini or Chavez or to be seen by them. Passing by, she saw no one.

Adele Kerr greeted her warmly at the door of the cottage. "I'm glad you've come. I've just made some fudge squares I want you to taste and tell me how you like them."

Carolyn was a bit overwhelmed by the domesticity of the elderly woman. How could she talk of Cabrini in this peaceful atmosphere? The old woman showed her into the small living room of the cottage and served her the squares with some tea.

"William is over at the main house for a little," she said.

Carolyn was surprised. "Can he get around on his own?"

The old woman smiled. "He does here. He knows every inch of the grounds. In strange places he has to depend on me or whoever is acting as his guide. But once he has paced an area he is able to walk about on his own. You have no idea how he enjoys this small independence."

"I think it's wonderful for him," Carolyn said.

Adele Kerr asked, "Do you like the squares?"

They were very good, and Carolyn told her so. They were still talking of cooking and other domestic problems when William Kerr finally returned. The blind man moved carefully, using his walking stick to test the area in front of him.

Carolyn greeted him and he said, "It's nice to have you here again, Miss Collins. We don't have too many visitors." When he was safely seated Carolyn told him the reason for her call. She mentioned Beth's joining the Cabrini company and told of the magician's police record.

William Kerr frowned as he listened. When she finished, he said, "I must warn you Cabrini is not only my tenant but my friend. I have just come from talking with him."

Disappointment surged through her. "Then you refuse to believe any ill of him?"

"I find it difficult to believe I have made such an error in judgment."

"No one could blame you," Carolyn said.

"I'm not so sure about that," William Kerr told her solemnly. "But I am not too impressed by the evidence you bring me against him."

"I see," she said quietly.

"Your friend Beth has a right to try a stage career if she wishes, and surely working with such a noted star as Cabrini ought to be a thrilling experience."

"But if she is doing it against her will? If he has hypnotized her?"

"I don't believe he could do that."

"What do you think about the reports from the London Police?" she asked.

"They are too vague," the blind man said. "Mysterious types like Cabrini always are the central figures in various tall stories. I suspect that is the explanation in this case."

Carolyn felt defeated. "So you still feel he is innocent of any wrongdoing?"

"I'm afraid that is my position," William Kerr said, "though I also agree you are entitled to your own opinions. I will not hold them against you. Adele and I want you to remain our friend."

His sister nodded. "That is so true, Carolyn. You must be tolerant of us just as we'll be tolerant of what you think."

This was an entirely unsatisfactory conclusion to her visit, but she knew it was as much as she could hope for. The elderly two had closed their minds to the fact that Cabrini could be anything but a loyal and respected friend. She would have to find some other way of settling with the weird magician.

As she was about to leave, William Kerr said, "I have heard that Quentin Collins has returned. The villagers are all talking about it and the murder at Bar Harbor."

Carolyn turned from the door where she stood with Adele. "I fail to see the link between the two."

From his chair William Kerr made a slight gesture with his right hand. "The watchman's throat was ripped open. Quentin has several times been mentioned in connection with the werewolf legend."

"I regard that as another of those tall stories you spoke of earlier," Carolyn said in a cold voice.

The blind man chuckled. "So you choose to defend Quentin Collins just as I insist on defending Cabrini."

"I'm afraid we're not likely to agree," she said.

"At any rate we'll not quarrel about it," William Kerr said. "Goodnight, my dear. Come again soon."

Adele saw her out to the car. "You mustn't mind William," she said. "His blindness has made him very stubborn."

"It's all right," Carolyn said. Then after saying goodnight, she drove back to Collinwood. On the way she decided she'd not soon pay another visit to the Kerrs. It had been a difficult evening for all of them, and it had left her feeling depressed.

When she reached home she found Quentin standing near the path to the front door.

"What are you doing out so late alone?" he asked.

"I've been over to see the Kerrs," she said.

The young man was at once interested. "They're strangers to me. They haven't been here too long. When did they buy the place?"

"Three years ago. But they only come here for brief stays most of the time. They were away from here when you made your previous visit."

"So I haven't met them yet. What are they like?"

She considered. "They're wealthy and old. I suppose you'd call them stubborn in their views. At least William Kerr is. He's blind and that makes it more difficult for him."

"Tell me more," Quentin said.

"There's not much else to tell," she sighed. "I suppose they're really very nice. But I can't forgive them for bringing that Cabrini here and causing all this trouble. Perhaps there are some other things I don't like."

"Such as?"

Hesitating, she looked up at the young man in the shadow. "He talks about Collinwood in a way I don't approve of. He brings up all the legends in a rather mean way. But then, he is blind."

"I must meet this William Kerr and his sister. I can see you are of a mixed mind about them," Quentin said. "And by the way, I saw Barnabas earlier this evening. You were right. He does seem very well."

"You noticed the difference?" she asked eagerly.

"Impossible not to be aware of it," Quentin said. "I wish I could find a Dr. Julia Hoffman for my problems."

"Why don't you visit her clinic? She may have some suggestions."

"I doubt that very much," Quentin said. "But now it's late. I won't keep you any longer."

"I don't mind."

"Roger is bound to," Quentin told her, "and I'm in enough trouble with him as it is. Go inside before he wakes up and hears us."

Carolyn did as he asked. The next several days and nights passed without incident. Then Cabrini came to visit Carolyn's mother and set the date of the performance at Collinwood. During his visit Carolyn came downstairs and was unable to avoid a meeting with him.

The bald man was wearing one of his neat black suits. He rose and bowed to her formally. "I have missed you," he said. "Beth has been expecting you to come over to the barn and watch rehearsals."

"I haven't felt like it."

"I'm sorry you have been unwell," Cabrini said, at once assuming she had been physically ill. "I would like to have you join us for the final preparations. You must do the guillotine act."

Carolyn had previously talked this all out with Barnabas. He had advised her to carry on with the show even though it went against her grain. He had explained that in this way she could not only keep in touch with Beth but observe Cabrini at close range.

"Very well," she said. "I'll go over. What time do you plan to begin?"

The bald man smiled again. "At dusk. I'll expect you."

When the magician had gone Elizabeth gave Carolyn a look of gratitude. "I'm glad you agreed to stay with the show. After all Cabrini's kindness to me I would have been embarrassed if you hadn't."

"I'm not doing it for his sake or for yours," Carolyn told her. She did not explain that her only motive was to try and rescue Beth from the clutches of the suave Cabrini.

The following morning the radio brought news of a second murder much resembling the first. This killing had taken place on the fringe of Collinsport. A wealthy female tourist was found dead in her expensive car. Her throat had been ripped open and all the expensive jewelry she'd been wearing had been stolen.

Young David was one of the most avid listeners to the account of the crime. When his father snapped the radio off the boy said, "Gee! Another murder! What do you think about it, Dad?"

Roger had gone white at the news. Now he told David, "I think you should go outside."

David frowned. "All you ever do is try to get rid of me!" he whined as he sulked out of the house.

When he was gone Roger turned to Carolyn and Elizabeth. "Where is Quentin?" he asked.

"I don't know," Elizabeth said nervously. "He didn't come home last night."

Roger gave them a knowing look. "Not likely. And the moon was full!"

"That doesn't mean anything!" Carolyn protested, though she was sick with fear for Quentin at the news.

Roger curled a thin lip. "I wish I could share your view," he said. "I can't. I'd expect the police to be here after Quentin before the morning is over. We can only hope he's gone away. This time he's really in trouble."

Carolyn said, "We should be the last to place any blame on him!"

Roger started for the door. "As if that would make any difference," he said. And he left for his office in the village.

Elizabeth looked as if she might faint. "Where do you suppose Quentin is?"

"He could be in Bangor or Boston," she said. "He often travels around."

"Let us hope he can prove he was somewhere else," her mother ventured nervously. "I'm afraid Roger is right. The villagers will start all that werewolf nonsense again."

Carolyn told her mother, "I'm going to the old house to see Barnabas. I want to find out what he thinks."

It was a warm, sunny morning. Carolyn hurried along the path past the stables and outbuildings which led to the old house. She couldn't wait to see Barnabas and hear what he had to say about this second murder. As she drew closer to the old house she was suddenly aware of a car parked in front of it. And as she came up to the car she felt panic surge through her. It was a State Police car! Barnabas had unexpected visitors!

CHAPTER 7

At the sight of the police car Carolyn halted and debated what she should do. While she wasn't sure why the police had come to interview Barnabas she supposed it had something to do with the murder. But why should they suspect him? She could understand their interest in Quentin, but Barnabas had never been associated with any murders in which throats had been ripped open.

Yet the fact remained the police were there. She didn't want to return to Collinwood nor did she wish to appear while Barnabas was being questioned. The only thing she could do was hide somewhere outside the house until the officers left. With this in mind she moved toward the rear of the house. It was then that she noticed the cellar entrance and remembered having used it long ago. If it should be open she could go down there and wait.

She examined the door closely and saw the lock had been removed. She tried the knob. It turned easily and she went inside. Carefully closing the door after her she stood in the damp, dark cellar. Memories of other days came rushing back to her as she groped her way along the earthen floor toward the back of the building and a door leading to a room which she would always remember.

In a moment she'd found the door and opened it. And once again she was in the cellar chamber that had housed the coffin in which Barnabas rested during the daylight hours. She peered through the murky shadows of the cold room and was able to make out the vague outline of the casket. It was still there in the corner!

She would never forget the first time she had entered this hidden room, then lighted by candles. She'd seen a gray coffin. And when she'd drawn close, she'd had the shock of discovering Barnabas in the velvet-lined box, his face placid as though in death. It had seemed to her she would never have such a terrifying moment again. Now she was not so certain!

She lingered in the dark room a few minutes longer, thankful that Barnabas had been restored to normalcy but wondering what might be going on upstairs. She was still standing there when the sound of footsteps coming towards her along the cellar floor sent a chill up her spine.

A moment later a flashlight beamed in her face. "So this is where you are," Barnabas said.

She gave a deep sigh of relief. "I didn't know you until you spoke. How did you know I was down here?"

"Willie saw you come in this way while I was busy with the police."

"The police have gone?"

"Yes."

"I saw them and it upset me. I couldn't imagine why they should be bothering you."

"You've heard about the second murder?"

"Yes. It's horrible!"

"They were looking for information about Quentin, mostly. But they also wanted to know about my movements."

She stared at him in dismay. "They can't think you had anything to do with it."

"They had questions to ask me."

"Were you able to satisfy them?"

"I hope so," Barnabas said in a bitter voice. "But you never can be sure." He glanced around the room. "I see no reason why we should remain down here. This is no longer my secret resting place."

"I'm grateful for that."

Barnabas beamed the flashlight on the coffin. "Sometimes I find myself longing for the escape that casket offered me. I was able to seek refuge from the world for hours at a time."

She gazed up at his gaunt, handsome face. "Surely you wouldn't prefer an existence like that to a normal life."

"In many ways no," he agreed with a grim smile. "But there are times when reality can be as horrible as the phantom world. I feel this may be one of them."

"You mustn't be discouraged."

"No," he agreed. "I mustn't." He guided her out of the room and along the blackness of the moldy cellar to the steep stone steps which led to the ground floor. When they reached the hallway he took her into the living room.

She sat down and asked, "What did the police say to you?"

"They asked me where I'd been last night," Barnabas told her. "Luckily I was able to give a satisfactory report of my evening's activities."

"What else?"

"They brought up the rumors about my having been a vampire. And they mentioned attacks in which young women had been bitten on their throats and robbed of blood."

"Nothing was ever proven against you!"

"Nothing definite," he amended her words. "But many of the attacks took place while I was in the area. I assume I'm still regarded as a suspicious person."

"At least you don't hide away during the daylight hours as you used to or prowl the cemeteries at night," she said. "They must have seen that you are as normal as anyone."

Barnabas smiled bitterly. "I think they were disappointed not to find me enjoying the sleep of the living dead in my casket. It ruined their case against me."

"Good," she said. "What about Quentin?"

"I'm afraid that's another story."

"It could be bad for him, couldn't it?"

"Unless he is able to come up with an ironclad alibi I expect they'll be placing him under arrest for the murders before the day is over."

"They really talked that way?"

"Yes. They started in on the werewolf business. They don't believe he actually changes into a werewolf as the legend goes. They think it's all in his mind. That at certain phases of the moon he believes himself to be a werewolf and behaves like one."

Her eyes met his. "You know better."

"Yes. I know better," Barnabas agreed. "Long ago I witnessed the transformation in him. It's not a thing I'd care to see again. Nor does he have any control over it."

"Regardless of that I'm sure he isn't committing the murders."

"He'd better have a good story to cover last night."

"He wasn't at Collinwood."

"So none of you can speak for him. That's bad."

"No."

"It seems we'll just have to wait and see what happens," Barnabas said with a sigh. "But they'll be back and they'll be questioning everyone, probably you along with the rest of us."

"I have nothing to hide."

"What's been happening with you?"

She looked unhappy. "Beth is still at Kerrhaven with the Cabrini troupe. And now he wants me to go over. It is getting near the date for the outdoor show."

"I'd almost forgotten," Barnabas said. "You're going?"

"You told me I should."

"I think it's a good idea. Who knows what you may discover?"

"I'm terrified at the thought of going there alone."

"He won't dare harm you."

"I'm not so sure of that. Won't you come along with me?"

Barnabas hesitated. "Would you feel safer?"

"Yes."

"It may put Cabrini more on his guard," he warned her.

"It will also give you an excuse to see what is going on over there."

"That is true," he admitted.

Carolyn said, "He wants me to go there at dusk tonight."

"I'll meet you in time to get there."

"Good." She sighed with relief.

"If you see Quentin before I do," Barnabas told her, "you'd better warn him that the police have been here and will be back."

"As soon as he hears about the murder he'll know that," she said. "I have an idea we won't see him again. He may have left for good."

"He has if he's wise," Barnabas said grimly. "I'll walk back as far as Collinwood with you. Then I'm going to the village to find out more about the killing."

It was a day of strain for everyone at Collinwood. Carolyn's mother was dreadfully upset and had gone so far as sending David to spend a few days with friends in Ellsworth. She hoped in this way to spare the boy from the unhappy scandal. Roger seemed to expect the worst and had been quick to agree to the plan.

Before dinner they gathered in the living room to discuss the situation over sherry.

Standing with Carolyn and her mother by the fireplace, Roger warned them, "This could be the worst thing that's ever happened to us here. Two murders and Quentin probably guilty of both of them."

Elizabeth, pale and nervous, protested, "I'm sure Quentin didn't rob that hotel safe or take that unfortunate woman's jewels."

"Why?" Roger asked sharply.

"He has no need to rob anyone. He was left independently wealthy. You know that."

"Wealth can be lost," Roger told her. "He may have made bad investments or simply wasted his inheritance. There's no reason why he couldn't be desperate for money."

Carolyn felt she should speak up on Quentin's behalf. "Aside from the money part, I just can't see Quentin as a murderer."

Roger's look was grim. "The police can."

"They're grasping at any straw to find the murderer," she said.

"That's true," her mother agreed.

"You can both stand up for Quentin all you like, now," Roger said. "But you'll share his shame if he's proven guilty later."

"He may not even have been in the village last night," Carolyn said. "He's certainly not here now."

"The police think he fled after the murder," Roger said.

Elizabeth gave her brother a worried glance. "I hope you didn't take sides with the police against Quentin. You surely attempted to defend the family name."

Roger looked uneasy. He stared at his half-empty sherry glass. "Naturally I tried to dismiss the whole business. But I couldn't argue about Quentin having been under suspicion before. They even brought up Barnabas."

"Barnabas is in the clear," Carolyn told her uncle. "He was able to account for his time last night."

"I know that," Roger said with a hint of annoyance. "I was merely trying to make it plain that the police are suspicious of all of us here."

Elizabeth sighed. "There's no use worrying this way. There's so little we can do. We may as well have dinner."

But the mood in the big, wood-paneled dining room was as gloomy as its shadowed atmosphere. Elizabeth preferred candlelight for the table and so they sat in the murky light in almost complete silence. None of them ate much. They were merely going through the motions of having dinner.

Such was the mood when another figure suddenly appeared in the room. It was Quentin! At the sight of him Roger jumped up from the table. Carolyn and her mother were equally startled. Roger demanded irately, "What are you doing back here?"

Quentin looked mildly surprised. He was dressed in white trousers and a blue blazer and appeared extremely neat and unperturbed. He seemed to be anything but a killer on the run.

"Why shouldn't I be here?"

Roger looked as if he might choke. "You've heard about the latest murder?"

"Yes," Quentin said.

"And you're not alarmed?"

"Why should I be?"

Roger crushed his napkin and threw it down on the table angrily. He told Quentin, "You don't need to have me spell it out. They think you are the killer."

"Let them," Quentin said.

Elizabeth got up from her chair. "The police have been here. They've also questioned Barnabas about you and they talked to Roger at his office."

Quentin gave Roger a disdainful glance. "I can imagine they really got a good report on me from you, Roger."

"I said nothing that wasn't true!" Roger snapped.

Carolyn had risen at the same time as her mother and now she went over to the young man. "Where were you last night, Quentin?"

"Visiting someone."

"Can you prove it? You'll have to if you are to convince the police of your innocence."

"Were you in the village at all?" Elizabeth asked.

"No."

For the first time Roger's rage visibly subsided and he looked at the quiet young man with new interest. "Are you saying you can actually prove that you weren't in Collinsport when the murder happened?"

"I believe so," Quentin said coolly.

"Either you can or you can't," Roger said. "Can't you give a straight answer?"

Carolyn turned on her uncle. "He already has."

Roger took a deep breath before he asked Quentin, "Would it be too much if I were to ask you to tell me exactly where you were last night? And who can vouch for it?"

Quentin seemed amused by Roger's anxiety. He said, "Would you believe me if I did tell you?"

Carolyn said, "Please tell us. We all want to know."

"Very well," the young man said. "I drove to Dr. Julia Hoffman's clinic nearly a hundred miles from here. I had a long consultation with her and Professor Stokes. It lasted until late at night. They persuaded me to take certain tests and remain in the clinic for further examinations this morning. I heard about the murders on the noon news broadcast and decided to come back."

Roger's eyebrows lifted. "You were at the clinic all evening and all last night?"

"Yes," Quentin said. "I shared a room with another patient. So I'll have no trouble proving it."

Roger gave a great sigh and sank into his chair at the head of the table. He looked completely exhausted, but demanded of Quentin, "Why didn't you tell us that when you first arrived?"

Quentin shrugged. "You seemed to be enjoying the idea that I was a murderer so much I didn't think I should spoil it for you."

Roger sat up angrily. "You deliberately led me on!"

Elizabeth gave her brother a placating look. "It doesn't matter.

The important thing is we know Quentin had nothing to do with the murder. I was sure of it anyway."

"Thank you, Elizabeth," Quentin said. He smiled at Carolyn. "I know you were on my side."

She returned a wan smile. "I did what I could. It has been a difficult day."

"I never want to go through another like it," Roger said. "Quentin, you must go directly into the village and tell the police your story."

"Why?" Quentin asked. "I'm in no danger."

"To clear this thing up," Roger said, rising again. "Why else?"

"It won't do anything to solve the murder," Quentin said. "It will only clear my name. I think I should let them come here to me."

"What?" Roger seemed unable to believe his ears.

"If they want to find out where I was let them come here," Quentin repeated. "In the meantime I'm hungry and I'd like to join you for dinner if I may."

Roger stared at him. "You're a pretty cool character, I must say."

"I have to be," Quentin told him as he accompanied Elizabeth back to the table. "I intend to find out who has been responsible for these killings. That requires a cool head."

Carolyn gave him a warning look. "Wouldn't it be better for you to leave here as soon as possible?"

"I agree," Roger said, as they all took their seats. "You can't tell what will happen next. And another time you may not have such a satisfactory alibi."

Quentin took a napkin and unfolded it on his lap. "It would seem to me I should be removed from suspicion in any future murders by the fact I couldn't have done this one. And the two to date have surely been linked."

"I agree the same criminal must have been responsible for both murders," Roger said.

"So that should leave me on the outside."

"I wouldn't be too sure. You never can tell how the police will feel."

During dinner Elizabeth made mention of the scheduled magical performance on the grounds of Collinwood, rousing her brother to anger once again.

Glaring at her, he said, "Surely you know that one of Cabrini's troupe must be responsible for these murders! Yet you have them here!"

Quentin smiled over his coffee cup. "A little while ago I was the logical suspect. You change your mind often."

Roger looked self-righteous. "I have always said one of those foreigners was to blame."

Elizabeth sighed. "I think you're just as wrong about that as you have been about Quentin and I don't care to argue about it further."

Seeing that his sister was serious, Roger Collins said no more. The meal ended and Carolyn managed to get a few minutes alone with Quentin in the living room before she left to meet Barnabas. "I think Uncle Roger is right about Cabrini. I'm very worried about Beth going to Kerrhaven."

"I realize that," Quentin said. "But our culprit may not be Cabrini himself. He has a lot of strange people around him. It will take time to sift them out."

"And is that what you propose to do?"

"Yes."

"I hope it doesn't take too long," she said. "I'm sure that if one of the group was proven guilty, Beth would leave them."

"Don't forget the police will be checking on them as well."

"What about you?" she asked. "Does Dr. Hoffman think she'll be able to help you?"

"My case is more complicated than she expected," Quentin said. "I'll not know until later. But she is willing to take me on as a patient."

"At least that's a beginning."

It was dusk when Carolyn left Collinwood. Quentin's arrival had left her feeling in a better mood. She waited on the front steps of the old mansion until she saw the familiar, tall figure in the Inverness cape come out of the shadows toward her.

She ran down to greet Barnabas. "I've been waiting to tell you what's happened," she said eagerly. As they walked toward Kerrhaven she gave him a brief account of all that had happened.

Barnabas listened gravely. When she'd finished, he said, "I'm glad Quentin is in the clear. I was worried about him."

"Do you think he should stay on here?"

"As long as he remains himself there is no problem. But if he should have one of his attacks and get involved in a crime it would be a different story."

"I know," she said worriedly. "He should go back to Dr. Hoffman's clinic and stay there until she's had a chance to give him some treatment."

"She may not be ready to begin yet. It takes a good deal of preparation in some cases," Barnabas explained.

"So Quentin could still get himself in serious trouble."

"There's that possibility."

It didn't take long until the lights of Kerrhaven showed ahead of them. There was also a new light over the entrance to the barn—the rehearsal would be taking place there.

Carolyn told Barnabas, "We may as well go directly to the barn.

Cabrini has a stage set up there."

"Very well," he said. "He won't be pleased to see me along."

"It makes no difference," she said. "I only hope I get a chance to talk to Beth."

"You should. Unless he deliberately keeps her away from the rehearsal."

"I doubt if he can do that," she said, "since he plans to use her in the show."

As they approached the entrance to the barn she saw the hunchback, Chavez, standing under the light. Upon seeing Barnabas, he hurried into the barn. His odd, furtive behavior at once put Carolyn on the alert.

Barnabas had also noticed it. He glanced down at her with a grim smile and said, "I believe we are being announced."

"So it appears."

They entered the barn which was completely dark except for the lighted, though empty, stage. Cabrini suddenly appeared out of the shadows to greet them.

"You're right on time, Miss Collins," he said pleasantly. "And I see you have a visitor with you. Welcome, Mr. Collins." The smile he gave Barnabas was unconvincing.

"I felt I wanted company after this other murder in the village," she said.

"Distressing," Cabrini said. "I was discussing it with William Kerr this afternoon. He and his sister are just as shocked as I am."

Barnabas asked the magician, "Have you any theories about the crimes?"

The bald man gave him a piercing look. "I think it is the work of a local," he said. "Someone who knows the district well and who has lived here for a long while."

"Interesting," Barnabas said. "That, of course, eliminates all of your company."

"I have never even considered any of my people possible criminals." Turning to Carolyn he said, "We must begin the rehearsal. There is a good deal of ground to cover."

Carolyn accompanied the magician to the stage, leaving Barnabas in the darkness. Cabrini clapped his hands twice and the two girl assistants whom Carolyn had seen before wheeled out the guillotine. She was anxiously watching for Beth but there was no sign of her.

Cabrini smiled. "You know something about this illusion. It shouldn't be such a frightening experience for you this time."

"No," she said. "I'm prepared."

"Then we shall begin." Cabrini went through the routine of having the heavy blade cut through a huge turnip and cabbage before placing Carolyn's head under it. This time she knew there was no danger and remained calm as the blade came swooping down.

Cabrini told her to wait backstage for a few minutes and clapped his hands twice again. The expressionless girls wheeled the guillotine off replacing it with an illusion called "The Window of the Enchanted House." In this effect Cabrini used one of the girls behind a mounted window so that her shadow could be clearly seen. But when the window was opened she was no longer there. Cabrini closed the window and the shadow was seen again. He repeated several variations of this as the illusion continued.

As Carolyn watched the magician from the wings, she was unable to restrain her admiration for his smooth performance, even though she neither liked nor trusted him. She was giving the act her full attention when someone touched her arm.

She glanced around quickly and saw someone standing in the shadows beside her. She whispered excitedly, "Beth!"

Beth, looking haggard and afraid, said, "I had to speak to you."

"You look ill," Carolyn said with concern.a"What's happened?"

"I can't tell you now. No time," Beth whispered. "But I'm terribly afraid."

Carolyn studied her friend with distress. "You must get away from here. Leave with me tonight."

Panic was in Beth's voice as she answered, "I can't! I don't dare!"

CHAPTER 8

C arolyn was shocked. "He can't keep you here against your wishes!"
"I must stay," Beth insisted urgently. "I'll explain later!"

"But why? You look ill and you seem terrified."

"You'd find it hard to understand. If I left now it would be dangerous for both you and I."

Carolyn was about to ask her friend what she meant but Cabrini, who had finished the window illusion, was walking across the stage toward them. An expression of displeasure clouded his features. He came directly to Beth and fixed his eyes hypnotically on hers.

"I didn't expect you here so soon," he said.

"I came a few minutes early," Beth said awkwardly. Her eyes were on Cabrini's and she seemed to be gradually slipping into that strange, aloof state.

"Of course it doesn't really matter," the magician said with a cold smile. "It gave you a chance to speak to Miss Collins."

"Yes." Beth said weakly in a voice that was merely an echo of her familiar one.

Cabrini continued to stare at her. "I hope you have given a good report of us here. That you've told her how much you're enjoying this new work."

"I have," Beth agreed meekly.

Cabrini seemed satisfied. He turned to Carolyn. "I'm glad you two got together. You'll both be featured in the show at Collinwood."

Carolyn felt she must do something for Beth. She said, "Why couldn't Beth live at Collinwood and come over here every day to rehearse with your troupe?"

The magician shook his head. "I'm sure she prefers living here." He looked questioningly at the transfixed Beth. "Isn't that so, my dear?"

She nodded dazedly. "Yes. I prefer living here." Carolyn wanted to tell Cabrini she knew he was using his hypnotic powers on her friend and announce that she was taking Beth with her no matter what. But she knew she couldn't do this. As long as Beth meekly agreed with all Cabrini's suggestions everyone would think she was a willing apprentice of the magician. Even though Carolyn knew this wasn't so. Beth's frightened words had made her terror clear. But how could Carolyn prove it?

Cabrini gave Carolyn one of his suave smiles. "I won't need you any longer tonight," he said.

It was evident he was worried about what Beth might have said to her and was anxious to get her out of the way. Carolyn feigned a desire to be helpful. "I can stay longer if you like."

"No need. In fact, I see no reason why you should return again. You know the illusion well enough for the actual performance."

"Is that all I'll be doing?" she asked.

"Yes," Cabrini said. "I prefer to use my professional people for most of the effects."

"I see," she said quietly, turning to Beth in one last effort. "You're sure you don't want to come home with me?"

Beth avoided looking at her directly. "No," she said. "Thank you."

"I'll see you on your way, Miss Collins." Cabrini's tone was cold as he politely ordered Carolyn to leave.

She gave a final glance at Beth, then allowed Cabrini to see her down from the stage to the other end of the darkened barn where Barnabas stood waiting for her.

Cabrini said, somewhat stiffly, "Thank you for escorting Miss Collins. There is no need for you to remain any longer."

"I enjoyed what I saw," Barnabas told him. "You have a fascinating show."

"It will be even better with more rehearsal," Cabrini assured him.

Carolyn gave the illusionist a troubled look. "I don't think Beth Mayberry is well. She looks terribly haggard."

Cabrini showed no concern. "I think it was the stage lighting that made her appear pale. She's in excellent health."

"I find that hard to believe," she argued.

"I assure you it is true," Cabrini said. "You'll excuse me but I have a heavy load of work for the balance of the evening. Goodnight to you both."

When Carolyn and Barnabas were outside, away from the barn Carolyn said, "He couldn't wait to be rid of us. And he certainly didn't want to talk about Beth."

Barnabas said, "Then you saw her?"

"Yes. At first she was very upset. Then he came and hypnotized her as he talked to her. She went into a kind of trance and just repeated everything he said."

"So she's being kept there by him, against her will."

"Yes."

Barnabas looked grim. "I wonder what it means? Perhaps he's attracted to her and this is his way of gaining control over her."

"He's evil," she said worriedly. "I know it." She glanced over and saw the lights of the Kerrs' cottage a short distance away. "I saw the Kerrs on my own as you advised," she said. "But they weren't helpful. William Kerr backs up Cabrini in everything."

"That creates a nasty situation."

"What can we do?"

"Let us wait until after Cabrini gives his performance at Collinwood," Barnabas suggested.

"You'll have a better chance to talk to Beth then. And maybe the truth of whatever is going on will be revealed."

"It's a small hope."

"It's all we have," Barnabas said as they began the walk back to Collinwood.

But Carolyn could not put Beth's terrified look out of her mind. "Something has frightened her."

"Probably Cabrini. I have an idea he can be cruel when the situation calls for it."

"I think so too," she agreed.

"I'm still working on getting information about him. It may come to us from an unexpected source."

This aroused her curiosity. "Where?" she asked.

"I can't tell you yet," Barnabas said mysteriously. "But I'll let you know as soon as I have anything definite."

"I hope it will be soon."

Barnabas saw Carolyn to the front door of Collinwood and kissed her goodnight. He waited until she was safely inside and then went on his way. When she entered the hall, Quentin was waiting for her in the semi-darkness.

With a knowing smile he said, "I watched your tender love scene with Cousin Barnabas."

Carolyn blushed. "That wasn't very nice of you!"

"I meant no harm," the young man assured her, "Though I must admit it made me a bit jealous."

"Don't be ridiculous!" she protested.

He took on a mocking air of sadness. "Now there's my whole problem. No one takes me seriously."

"I do when you deserve it."

"And I don't now," he sighed. "Well, there it is. Aside from your romantic interlude with Barnabas, how did you make out tonight?"

"Cabrini was glad to see me leave," she said. She proceeded to tell Quentin all that had happened at Kerrhaven.

Quentin seemed shocked by her story. "Couldn't you find any way of getting this Beth out of there?"

"No."

"There must be a way," he insisted.

"Barnabas suggested we wait until the show comes here and then try to convince her to remain here."

"Before you can manage that you'll have to separate her from Cabrini. If he's anywhere near her he'll use more hypnosis to keep control of her."

"Why is he so determined to do that?"

"A good question," Quentin said. "There could be a number of answers. Beth is not a poor girl. Cabrini might be interested in her money."

"I'm sorry he ever saw her," Carolyn said unhappily. "Then he wouldn't have had this chance to ruin her life."

"By the way, the police were here after you left," Quentin said. "I talked with them, so Uncle Roger ought to be satisfied."

"What did they say?"

"They believe the two murders were done by the same person. They phoned Dr. Hoffman before they left to confirm what I'd told them. So I'm in the clear for now."

"I'm glad," she said sincerely.

"I knew you would be," Quentin smiled. "I'm sure Roger is more than a little disappointed."

"He isn't all bad," she said. "It's just that he's so conservative and stuffy. But he sometimes comes around to a more liberal point of view."

"I'm working on him now," Quentin said, "trying to make him more friendly to Barnabas and me."

"I hope you succeed," Carolyn said. She knew there was always the chance that Barnabas might have a recurrence of his trouble. If it came at this time of violent murder he would be in as precarious a position as Quentin.

In her dreams that night, Carolyn again saw the haggard, frightened face of Beth. She tried to talk to her but Beth seemed suddenly to lose her voice. She stood speechless while Carolyn pleaded with her to say what was troubling her. At this moment, Cabrini, flushed with anger, came on the scene and roughly hurled Carolyn down. He stood over her as she crouched on the floor, his mad hypnotic eyes staring at her, casting a spell so powerful that she gradually lost consciousness. With this unconsciousness came the end of her dream.

The following day proved more unpleasant than her dreams. William Kerr and his sister paid a visit to Collinwood in the afternoon. And as soon as Carolyn saw their troubled faces she knew there was some new crisis.

"I have come to ask your opinion about something, Mrs. Stoddard," the blind man immediately began.

Carolyn's mother gazed at him sympathetically. "I'll be glad to do anything I can."

"Thank you." Kerr's placid tone revealed no emotion. "A disturbing thing took place at Kerrhaven last night."

"Oh?" Elizabeth glanced at Carolyn who was listening attentively.

"Yes," Kerr continued. "And Cabrini has placed it before me to make a decision."

"Please go on," Elizabeth urged him as he hesitated.

"One of Cabrini's girl assistants was attacked in a most mysterious fashion," Kerr suddenly blurted out.

"Was it Beth Mayberry?" Carolyn asked anxiously.

Kerr shook his head. "No. It was one of the foreign girls who came here with him."

"Was she badly hurt?" Elizabeth inquired in a tense voice.

"She's alive and seems well enough this morning." Adele Kerr spoke for the first time.

"That's not the point, Adele," her brother said irritably. "The strange thing is the manner in which she was attacked."

Carolyn felt herself begin to tremble. She was afraid she knew what she was about to hear. "What happened to the girl?"

"She was walking from the barn to the house when someone came out of the bushes at her," Kerr began nervously. "Before she knew what was happening this figure in black seized her and sank his teeth into her throat. The red marks are still there as proof. This creature must have somehow drained blood from her. She became weaker and weaker until she fainted. When she came to, she was on the ground near our cottage, but she made her way back to the main house and told Cabrini her story."

Adele Kerr's elderly features were distorted by fear. "What my brother is trying to tell you is that this seems like a vampire attack. The sort that happened here some time ago."

"I think the entire story is exaggerated," Elizabeth said. "We do not believe in vampires here."

"That's very convenient for you," William Kerr said sternly. "But I have heard strange stories about your cousin from England. There are rumors that he is a vampire."

"They're wrong!" Carolyn protested.

"I hope so," the blind man said. "But Cabrini is most upset. He wanted to turn the matter over to the State Police. I prevailed upon him to let me take care of it in my own way. That is why I have come directly to you as a friend and a neighbor. I want your honest reply as to whether Barnabas Collins still suffers from the vampire curse?"

Elizabeth had gone pale. "Nothing was ever proven about Barnabas."

Carolyn was also in a panic. Either Cabrini had decided to fake a charge against Barnabas or the handsome Britisher had actually fallen under the vampire curse again and made the attack. Either way it was bad for Barnabas.

"Couldn't the girl have been mistaken?"

"There was no mistake," Kerr said sternly. "I want to protect your good name as well as I can, but I must know the truth."

"There's nothing we can tell you," Elizabeth said.

Adele Kerr leaned forward nervously. "But isn't it true that this Barnabas is descended from a man who was banished from Collinwood for being a vampire?"

"The family legends are more fancy than truth," Carolyn told her.

The white-haired man raised his stooped body out of the easy chair. "It seems we are not going to get any help here."

"I'm sorry," Carolyn's mother said, "but we can't tell you any more."

"I'm going to see this is hushed up only because of my friendship with all of you. But if Cabrini reports any more such incidents I can only encourage him to notify the police."

Adele Kerr stood at her brother's side. "We can pray it won't be repeated."

"I'm sure it won't," Elizabeth said, and she showed the visitors out.

It seemed to Carolyn that her world was collapsing around her. In all their troubles she had relied on the new Barnabas Collins. Now it seemed likely that Barnabas had been overtaken by that ancient curse!

Her mother came back into the living room and slumped into a chair. "What do you make of it?" she asked, her voice full of despair.

Carolyn shook her head. "I don't know."

"William Kerr is our friend. He only wants to protect us."

"That is true."

"It's Cabrini," Elizabeth said worriedly. "But if one of his assistants was attacked in the way William Kerr described, Cabrini has a right to be angry."

"If the attack really took place."

"Do you think it mightn't have?"

"Cabrini could have schemed the whole thing. I don't think he liked the fact that Barnabas went to the rehearsal with me last night. He was probably worried that Beth told me some of his secrets, and that I told Barnabas."

Elizabeth stared at her. "Are you suggesting that Cabrini devised a plot to hurt Barnabas?"

"Yes."

"Would the girl be willing to lie about it?"

"He has hypnotic control over the people in his company. They'll say anything he tells them to."

Elizabeth looked doubtful. "I'm still inclined to think we're being unfair to Cabrini. But there's a way to be certain."

Carolyn knew what her mother was thinking. "You mean find out about Barnabas?"

"Yes," her mother said quietly. "He hasn't been around today."

"Sometimes we don't see him until the evening."

"When he was ill we only saw him between dusk and dawn," Elizabeth reminded her.

Carolyn replied with a defiance she didn't really feel, "I'm sure he hasn't gone back to that state again."

"You'd better make sure, and quickly," Elizabeth said. "If it is trouble we'll have to get word to Roger at once."

"I'll go to the old house now," Carolyn said, starting out the door.

Her mother called after her, "Be careful!"

The words sent a chill through the girl. The mere thought that she should be afraid of Barnabas was shattering. Barnabas, whom she loved and who she was sure cared for her. Fate couldn't be so cruel as to have made of him a living dead man again.

Carolyn hurried out into the summer sunshine, her eyes blurred with tears. When she reached the old house she mounted the stone steps and knocked on the oaken door. There was no reply. She tried the door. It was locked. She pounded on the door with growing desperation.

No one was answering. Feeling that her worst fears were being confirmed she slowly descended the steps and went around to the side of the house. There was that door —the one that led to the dark regions under the ancient house. The coffin in which Barnabas had slept every day while he suffered the vampire curse was here. Was he back in that coffin now?

If he had made the attack the previous night she knew he would be in the cellar now, sleeping the sleep of death, satiated with the blood which enabled him to survive as a monster of the dark hours. Feeling sick with fear, Carolyn opened the cellar door and ventured into the blackness. She crossed the damp floor and made her way to the door leading to the secret room.

Now the moment of torment had arrived. She hesitated at the door, unwilling to enter the room and make the discovery she feared awaited her. But she had no choice. She must know. Trembling, she opened the door and inched toward the coffin in the corner. She had a mental vision of Barnabas resting there, his hands folded on his chest. She could almost see his face through the shadows!

She bent over the casket, expecting to see that handsome, gaunt face. But the coffin was empty! It was like a reprieve! A sob of thankfulness escaped her parched throat as she turned away from the shadowy box of death. She was about to hurry from the room when she heard a footstep outside. She waited tensely.

Then Willie Loomis appeared in the doorway. He glared at her. "What are you doing here?"

"I came to find Barnabas."

"You should know better than to look for him here these days," the youth told her.

"I tried the door. No one answered."

"We were both out."

"Do you know where Barnabas is?"

"He's back now. He's upstairs."

"Thank you, Willie," she said hurriedly. "I must see him. I have to talk to him." She rushed past the astonished young man and made her way out of the cellar.

She was sobbing when she found Barnabas in the living room. She ran into his arms and pressed herself to him. For a moment she was unable to say anything. He patted her gently and tried to calm her.

"What's this all about?" he asked.

Stifling her sobs, she told him what she had just done. "Forgive me for being so weak and foolish," she apologized, finally in control of her emotions.

Barnabas studied her with gentle eyes. "I find nothing weak or foolish about you," he said. "I'd say you were loyal and wise. I certainly didn't attack the girl. So there's only one explanation. Cabrini cooked this up to make trouble for me."

"I knew it!" she exclaimed bitterly. "But why is he trying so hard?"

"He's apparently afraid of me for some reason."

"He's guilty of Heaven knows what," Carolyn said, searching for an answer. "And he's made poor old William Kerr believe everything he says."

"Kerr is obviously his dupe," Barnabas agreed. "I can't imagine why an otherwise smart man would be taken in by a character like Cabrini."

"Cabrini is very smooth," she said. "He even has mother convinced he's all right."

Barnabas looked at her with a grim smile. "And he had you at the point where you were peeking in coffins to see if I was there. You're right.

He's a wily character."

"We're safe for the present," Carolyn sighed. "Kerr talked him out of going to the police. But if he manufactures another attack the trouble will really start."

"That's the threat he's holding over us," Barnabas said. "He's done this to warn us to leave him alone. Not to interfere with his evil plans."

"It looks as if that's true. Quentin is in the clear, and now Cabrini is starting a campaign against you."

"As long as we know his charges aren't true we needn't worry too much."

"He must be desperate to work out such devious schemes."

"Probably. But for now we'll simply have to go on playing a waiting game."

But Carolyn wasn't patient by nature and waiting tried her nerves. She was terribly concerned about Beth, especially since there was no further word from her. As the evening of the magic show at Collinwood drew near, the clamor about the murders gradually died down. It seemed that everyone but the police had forgotten about them.

Quentin went off to see Dr. Julia Hoffman again and was away from Collinwood for more than a week. Elizabeth had arranged for David to stay in Ellsworth until the evening of the magic performance. She knew that to rob him of that experience would be to break his young heart.

During the remaining days before the event, both Elizabeth and Carolyn threw themselves feverishly into the preparations for the show in an effort to forget the other pressures that still bore down on them. Carolyn was in charge of the ticket sale and the local people, eager to see the legendary Cabrini, bought up most of the tickets a full week before the performance date.

Elizabeth managed the entire affair and Barnabas acted as a foreman for the carpenters erecting the temporary stage out beyond the rose gardens. Chairs were brought from the village hall and kept in the stables until the big evening. Excitement in the village and at Collinwood was at a feverish pitch when the day of the show finally arrived.

It was fine and warm and the evening would be ideal for the entertainment. When Cabrini came over in the afternoon to check the stage and lighting, Barnabas discreetly kept out of the way. The magician, after approving the set-up, announced that the vans carrying the company and properties would be there shortly after seven. The performance would begin as soon as it was dark.

Barnabas was overseeing the hanging of the black stage drapes when Roger returned from the village. Seeing the chairs set out on the lawn and the trampled, ruined grass in the vicinity of the stage where the workmen had been, he let out a groan. "We won't have any lawn left after tonight."

"I don't think it will be all that bad," Barnabas told him with a wink for Carolyn who was standing by.

"Look at it now!" Roger wailed. "And think of what it will be like after those vans roll up and an audience of three or four hundred crushes the grass."

Carolyn said, "Think of the money this show will raise for the hospital fund."

"It will cost me at least an equal amount to restore the lawns," Roger fumed. "I would have been better off to give them a donation and get it over with." He stomped into the house, leaving Barnabas and Carolyn to smile at his anger.

David arrived in time for dinner and like everyone else, was becoming extremely excited. Carolyn was especially on edge. Not only was she going to take part in the magic performance for the first time but she hoped to be able to talk to Beth again. If things worked out as she hoped, Beth might be persuaded to leave Cabrini and return to Collinwood.

She put on the smart yellow dress Cabrini had approved for the show and went down to get ready for the performance. Many chairs were already filled, even though it would be some time until dusk. Cabrini's vans had arrived and the front curtain closed. Behind the scenes his company worked to set up the show.

Carolyn immediately went backstage to seek out the magician. She saw Chavez busily directing the stage crew in setting out various props, and the two girl assistants were preparing some of the smaller effects. They paid no attention to Carolyn as she passed them. And she found herself wondering which one of them had made the false accusation against Barnabas.

Carolyn wandered among the confusion backstage, searching for Beth or Cabrini, finding neither of them. She moved uneasily to the side of the temporary stage from which point she could get a view of the audience and was heartened to see Barnabas seated in the front with David. Her Uncle Roger and her mother were still taking tickets at the other end of the lawn as more people continued to arrive. It looked like there would be a full house.

Dusk was settling and the show would soon begin. Carolyn went to the backstage area once more. This time she met Cabrini almost immediately. His face was taut with tension and he almost looked right past her.

"Where is Beth?" she asked him.

"I don't know," the magician replied. "She came over with us, but now she seems to have disappeared. I've been looking everywhere for her. She's completely dropped out of sight."

CHAPTER 9

Carolyn felt an increasing uneasiness as she stared at the magician. He was pretending Beth had been there and vanished, but Carolyn was certain that Cabrini had been careful not to bring Beth along in order to avoid any chance of her deserting him.

"It's odd that I didn't see Beth earlier."

The bald man eyed her coldly. "She was here. She came in my car. If she doesn't return I'll have to assign her part in the show to one of the other girls."

"If she was here she can't be very far away."

"I hope not," Cabrini said. "We'll be starting the show in a few minutes and I'll want you available toward the end of the first half."

Carolyn nodded. "I'll take a look out front. She may have gone there to speak with my mother."

"If you find her send her to me at once," Cabrini said, and walked away to give Chavez instructions about the stage lighting.

Carolyn left the backstage area to walk along the lawn to where her mother and Roger were taking tickets. She was impressed by the crowd that had assembled on this pleasant summer night. Nearly all the several hundred chairs were filled.

When she reached the entrance gate, Roger was taking the tickets and her mother was chatting with Adele Kerr, who looked especially dressed up for the occasion.

The prim Adele was saying, "I'm sorry William wasn't able to attend with me, but he has a bad headache. And it's not easy for him to follow a performance such as this without his sight."

"It wouldn't entertain him much at all," Elizabeth agreed.

"But he would have been here if he hadn't taken ill," the elderly woman continued. And with a smile for Carolyn, she went on to find a chair.

As soon as she was alone with her mother Carolyn said, "There's something funny going on. Beth isn't anywhere to be found and Cabrini claims he brought her over in his car."

Elizabeth raised her eyebrows. "But she's to take part in the show."

"She was to," Carolyn said bitterly. "Now Cabrini is talking about turning over her role to one of the other girls. I don't think he allowed her to come. He didn't want to risk our persuading her to remain here."

"Surely that's not so," Elizabeth insisted, trying not to believe her daughter's words.

"It's the way I see it. And if I don't see Beth tonight I'm going over to Kerrhaven tomorrow and demand to be allowed to talk to her."

Elizabeth sighed. "Why must you always look for trouble? It's very likely she'll turn up for the show."

Roger had evidently heard their tense conversation as he hurried over to them and asked, "What's wrong now?"

Carolyn related her conversation with the magician. "I think Cabrini is keeping her away from us deliberately."

"I wouldn't be surprised," Roger said with a scowl. "I'll be glad when tonight is over. I don't want that fellow around here. On top of everything else, it will cost me more than we'll make tonight to restore this lawn to its former state."

Carolyn's mother turned to him, annoyed. "You're always complaining, Roger. Nothing ever pleases you!"

"I can promise you this doesn't," he snapped, leaving her to greet an arriving couple.

Elizabeth looked at Carolyn despairingly. "You see what I have to put up with all the time."

"In a way I sympathize with Uncle Roger. I think we would have been wiser not to have had this show. But I must go backstage now. I'm on during the first half of the performance."

She walked back toward the stage. It was dark now and the floodlights had been turned on the front curtain, which carried Cabrini's name in large gold letters. There was an air of expectancy among the audience seated under the starry sky. Carolyn felt some of the excitement herself even though she was still worried about Beth.

Backstage she saw Cabrini in his dress suit and top hat, ready to make his entrance and open the show. The assistants were in the rear, waiting to do the tasks assigned to them. On a given signal the curtain was drawn and Cabrini moved onto the stage with a swagger and a smile, twirling his white cane in his white-gloved hands.

Chavez was presiding over a complicated sound system which was pouring out background music for the show. The opening number was bright. Carolyn watched from the side as Cabrini pulled off his white gloves and crumpled them into a ball. At once the gloves turned into a white dove. He then held the dove gently in one hand as he tapped his white cane on the floor with the other. In a twinkling the cane had become a small ornamental cage. He slipped the dove into the cage and triumphantly held it up for the audience to see.

Before the applause ended one of the girl assistants had taken the bird and cage from the stage. Now Cabrini removed his top hat and removed from it a giant bouquet of red roses. Then he began drawing dozens of loose flowers from the hat. Finally, he collapsed the hat and it vanished. He moved on to his silk tricks and Carolyn could tell that Cabrini had won over the audience. They were delighting in everything he did.

There was no question that he was an expert showman. His vitality was astonishing since he was far from young. He worked for another twenty minutes, while Chavez kept changing the music to suit the presentation on the stage. The hunchback was so involved with his task that he didn't raise his head from the record turntable except to make sure the music was on cue.

Now Cabrini began to introduce his illusions. He did a levitation trick using one of the female assistants. Shortly after that Chavez looked at Carolyn for the first time and ordered her to be ready to go on. She was trembling as she waited in the wings for the guillotine to be wheeled on stage. Soon Cabrini would smile and signal her to appear.

The two girls brought the guillotine to its place in center stage as Cabrini beckoned to her. She went on and the audience responded to the appearance of a local girl by giving her a loud ovation. Now Cabrini went through the routine they'd rehearsed. He split the turnip and the lettuce with the sharp steel blade and then put Carolyn's head on the block. She could fairly sense the people in the audience holding their breath as the moment came for the blade to descend. When it did she was aware of their gasps. When she emerged unhurt, they applauded louder than ever before.

This marked the conclusion of the first half of the show. When the magician had taken several curtain calls and the curtain had come down for intermission, he walked over to Carolyn. "You did well."

"Thank you," she managed to reply. She was numb from the excitement. But even now she began to wonder about Beth.

It seemed that Cabrini must have been reading her thoughts. "If Beth doesn't show up in a few minutes I'll have to use a substitute for her," he said too casually.

"I don't understand it," Carolyn said, shaking her head.

"Nor do I," he said, a scowl on his bony face. "I didn't think she was the type to let me down."

"There must be a reason."

"I'd like to know it," Cabrini said as he walked away.

Now that her part in the show was over there was no reason for Carolyn to remain backstage. She made her way out around the edge of the stage and along the lawn without going near the rows of spectators. As she reached the rear of the assemblage she met Barnabas and David walking in the shadows.

David came racing up to her with boyish enthusiasm. "You were great!" he shouted. "I thought for sure you'd lose your head."

She smiled at him. "So did I the first time we rehearsed."

Barnabas was amused. "I had no idea you were such a competent actress."

"I had hardly anything to do. Cabrini is the whole show."

"You did well," Barnabas said. "But you're right. There is no question that Cabrini is an unusually adept performer."

"When will Beth be on?" David asked excitedly.

She gave the boy a worried glance. "I don't think she'll be in the show tonight."

David looked disappointed. "Gosh, I wanted to see her."

"So did I," Barnabas said, his voice full of meaning. "What's happened?"

"She's nowhere to be found. Cabrini claims she was here and vanished."

"You haven't seen her?"

"No. And in my opinion he wouldn't let her come here. He's merely pretending to be baffled by her disappearance."

"It could be," Barnabas agreed. "He's very crafty."

"I've found that out," Carolyn said. "I'm going to find Beth tomorrow if she doesn't show up tonight. I'll go to Kerrhaven after her."

Barnabas looked at her knowingly. "He could easily arrange to spirit her away from Kerrhaven if it suited his purposes."

Suddenly, the sound system came on again and the floodlights fell on the curtain. Carolyn, Barnabas, and David took their seats as the second half of the show began with the illusion in which a girl seemed to turn into a skeleton then vanish. It was the trick she'd seen Beth rehearse, but the girl now being featured was not her friend. Carolyn was becoming more edgy.

The performance went on with Cabrini outdoing himself in an escape act. But while the audience remained enthusiastic, Carolyn found her thoughts wandering. She just couldn't concentrate on what was happening on the brightly lighted stage. When Cabrini produced a large "Good Night" banner from the air and the final curtain fell, she felt a true sense of relief.

The audience was generous in giving him curtain calls, the magician was enjoying every moment of the adulation. At last it was over and the curtain dropped for the final time as the audience began to disperse.

As David headed back for the house, Barnabas and Carolyn watched the people returning to their cars in the special area reserved for parking. "It's the largest audience I've ever seen locally," he commented.

"I know," she said. "I hate to think what the grounds will look like in daylight."

"Roger has already been making predictions about that… grim ones," Barnabas added with a smile.

"Mother wanted to have the show," she said. "I hope she's satisfied."

"She should be. It was quite a success."

"I'm thinking about Beth," Carolyn sighed. "And what has really happened to her." She glanced toward the stage and was surprised to see Roger and Cabrini coming to join them. Both men looked upset.

Roger was the first to speak as they approached. "Has either of you seen Beth Mayberry?"

"No," Carolyn told him, nervously looking at Cabrini.

"She's still missing?" Barnabas inquired.

Cabrini was wearing a black sweater and slacks, one of his work outfits. He now looked older and strained, not at all like the debonair, graceful performer who'd appeared on the stage such a short time before. It was as if all the energy had been drained out of him.

"I sent one of my people back to Kerrhaven," Cabrini said. "Beth isn't there so something must have happened to her. Or perhaps she has run off."

"I don't believe that," Carolyn said.

The magician shrugged. "She vanished after she came over here."

"In that case we should make a search of the house and grounds," Roger Collins offered. "She may be hiding somewhere."

"I agree. A search should be made," Cabrini said.

"It seems preposterous to me," Carolyn protested. "She's probably somewhere at Kerrhaven."

"No," Cabrini said curtly, "she most definitely is not."

Barnabas gave Carolyn a look of warning. "I can't see that it will do any harm to conduct a search of the grounds. At least it will settle whether she is here or not."

"I don't think she'll turn up here," Carolyn said.

"Why do you say that?" her Uncle Roger demanded irritably.

"Because it's what I feel." She looked directly at Cabrini. "It's what I know."

Cabrini looked grim. "I will have some of my people search this part of the grounds and perhaps someone more familiar with the other areas could look there."

"Of course we must organize the search properly," Roger said. "No need for a lot of senseless duplication. The best way is to assign everyone to a certain section."

"Can we help?" Barnabas asked.

Roger frowned. "I suppose so. You and Carolyn can take a look around your place. I'll assign you to that area. Be sure and report to me by the morning at the latest. And let us know at once if you should find Beth."

"Very well," Barnabas said. He and Carolyn left the two men to set out on their search. She knew he'd been eager to get away from Roger and the magician.

When they were completely alone she asked him, "What do you think about it?"

"It's hard to say. It could be part of the act you think Cabrini is putting on. I don't really expect to discover Beth at the old house."

"Nor do I." They were on the path that passed by the stables.

"Still, we couldn't not offer to cooperate," he pointed out.

"I feel as if I'm the victim of a practical joke," she complained. "Cabrini is sly. He'll carry this through as if he really thinks Beth is missing."

"More trouble for Roger," Barnabas said. "Now there'll be searchers all over the estate."

"And all for nothing," she said resignedly.

They reached the old house and the only one there was Willie. Under questioning from Barnabas, he told them he thought he had seen two people walking by the house earlier, heading for the ancient cemetery.

"You couldn't make out who it was?" Barnabas asked.

"No," the young man said. "At first I was sure it was you and Miss Carolyn. You often stroll around the grounds after dusk."

She asked, "Had the show begun yet?"

"I don't think so," Willie said. "I didn't hear the music until later."

Barnabas was frowning. "And you are sure these two vanished in the direction of the cemetery?"

"Yes," Willie said.

Barnabas turned to Carolyn. "Well, that's the end of it. It looks as if we'll have to stroll down to the cemetery. I'm glad that we have a starry night."

"Do you think we should bother? I think it's all a hoax."

"We can't be positive. I guess we'd better go down there and take a look."

"I can't imagine Beth's going there. And who could it have been with her?"

"Yes, who? That could be the answer to the whole mystery of her disappearance," Barnabas pointed out.

They left the old house, walking under the starry skies in the general direction of the cemetery. As they strolled they barely spoke at all. Both of them were tense. Carolyn was beginning to have qualms about Beth's safety. When they reached the open gate of the ancient burial ground, she suddenly was seized by a feeling of terror and could walk no further.

Barnabas stared at her in surprise. "What now?"

She gave him a frightened look. "I can't explain it, but I don't want to go any further."

His handsome face took on a baffled expression. "You're no stranger to this place."

"I know that."

"Yet you're afraid to enter the cemetery? Why?"

"I can only tell you that the thought of going in there makes me sick with fear."

Barnabas hesitated, then said, "Do you mind waiting here while I go on alone?"

"No."

"You're sure you'll be all right?"

"Yes. I'll wait right here for you."

Barnabas looked at Carolyn warmly. "I have to take a look in there after what Willie told us. But I'll only be a few minutes."

"It's all right," she said, but her teeth were chattering from sheer nervousness.

He touched a hand to her arm in an effort to comfort her. "I've seldom seen you in such a state."

"I can't help it," she said abjectly.

Barnabas sighed. "Well, I may as well get it over with and then see you back to Collinwood. You've had too many demands on your nerves today." He made his way into the ancient cemetery, whose gravestones were standing like silent sentinels.

She felt ridiculous for making such a scene, but she hadn't been able to force herself to go along with him. Somehow the isolated old cemetery she had visited so often had taken on an air of evil. She felt there was an unknown force lurking there. A force she didn't understand but one which terrified her.

She stood there under the stars, straining for some sign of Barnabas in the cemetery. But she couldn't see him. Every small sound in the night made her start. Beth's disappearance and now this unexplainable feeling had completely unraveled her nerves.

All at once she saw Barnabas's shadowy form as he moved among the gravestones. He was walking back toward her. She waited for his words, her heart pounding from fear.

"We have to see Roger at once," he said brusquely, taking her by the arm and starting to guide her across the field.

Taken aback by his haste, she stared up at him. "There is something you haven't told me. What is it?"

"Time enough later," he said, avoiding her eyes as his handsome face showed the strain of his ordeal.

"You must tell me now!"

He glanced at her worriedly. "You're better off not knowing."

She halted. "Tell me!"

He was torn by many emotions. Speaking with difficulty, he said, "I found Beth. In there."

"No!" She pressed a hand to her mouth.

His arm was around her. "You mustn't think about it."

"She's dead?" Carolyn said in a hoarse whisper.

"Yes."

"How?"

He eyed her with despair. "The same as the others. Her throat was slashed."

Carolyn felt a wave of nausea come over her, and then she fainted. When she opened her eyes again she was stretched out on a divan in the living room of the old house, and Barnabas was bending over her.

"You'll be all right now," he said.

She stared up at him. And then memory came flooding back. "Beth!" she sobbed brokenly.

He sat on the divan and cradled her in his arms. "There's no use in your going on that way. There's nothing you can do."

"It was Cabrini," she said, anger suddenly replacing her grief.

"We'll find that out."

"It has to be! Did you let them know?"

"Yes. Willie has gone with the message," Barnabas said in a taut voice. "I expect in a short time they'll all be swarming around here. The police will be taking charge."

She gave him a frightened look. "You can prove where you were all evening. You and David were together."

"Most of the time," he agreed.

"And Quentin is at Dr. Hoffman's clinic, so he's safely out of it."

"Unless he left the clinic and arrived here tonight without advising any of us," Barnabas said.

"Would he do that?" Carolyn was becoming anxious for the young man.

"You never can be sure. At any rate, we can suppose he didn't. So that eliminates Quentin."

"And it comes back to Cabrini."

Barnabas was thoughtful. "Or one of his troupe. Beth was a favorite of mine, though I knew her only briefly. I feel as terrible as you do about what has happened."

"We were like sisters," she murmured.

"This makes three murders."

Carolyn's eyes were wide. "I'm positive Cabrini murdered her or had her murdered to ensure her silence."

"Maybe," Barnabas said.

"I know it," she insisted.

"We'll find out in good time."

"How can you be so calm?"

"I'm not, really," Barnabas said. "I dislike the idea of being questioned by the police again more than you can guess. My own position is not that strong yet."

At once she felt sympathy for him. "Poor Barnabas," she whispered.

He got up and began to pace slowly back and forth. "I first have to find out if Quentin returned here or whether he is still with Dr. Hoffman."

"You have no phone here."

"No. There are no modern conveniences in this house," he said. "I have kept it the same as it was two centuries ago."

"You could phone from Collinwood," she suggested.

"I'd rather go into the village," he said worriedly. "I want to avoid the police until I have more information."

Carolyn got up from the divan. "Then we should leave before the police arrive."

"It would be best," he admitted, looking haggard. "But are you sure you feel well enough to drive to the village with me? Also, I may have to go somewhere else later."

"I don't want to leave you," she said decisively.

"Very well. I don't think we should waste any more time."

A few minutes later they were in Barnabas's station wagon, taking the old road to the village. He deliberately used this route to avoid meeting the police.

Sitting in the semi-darkness of the car's interior, Carolyn began to worry about this trip. "Won't they think you've run away? That you are afraid of being questioned?"

"Possibly."

"And you don't mind?"

"I have no choice," he said tautly.

She stared at him and saw the grim look on his handsome face, revealed by the car's dash lights. They were heading swiftly in the direction of the village while the car was being pounded by the rocks and ruts in the rough road.

"Where was she?" Carolyn asked suddenly.

"Behind one of the gravestones."

"Were there signs of a struggle?"

"Her eyes were staring," Barnabas said. "And her clothes were rumpled. I didn't make too complete an inspection of the area. Let the police do that."

She closed her eyes. "My poor Beth!"

"She was the third victim," Barnabas reminded her. "The police will be doubly eager to make an arrest now. Any arrest! That's why it's so important that Quentin should have remained at Dr. Hoffman's."

"What if he is still there?"

"I'll decide then what I should do next," Barnabas told her. "I'll probably take you back to Collinwood before I do anything."

"I only feel safe when I'm with you," she said sincerely. After what had happened to Beth she was terrified. Cabrini's stern, bony face haunted her.

They reached the village and Barnabas halted the car at the first public telephone booth. She remained in the car while he made the call. She watched anxiously as he stood talking. After a few minutes he hung up the receiver and got back into the car.

"Quentin left the clinic this morning," he said in a troubled voice. "He told Dr. Hoffman he was going to see a friend in Augusta. Let's hope he can prove he was there tonight."

CHAPTER 10

"What now?" Carolyn asked worriedly.

Barnabas gave her a thoughtful glance. "I'm driving to Julia Hoffman's clinic. She wants to tell me something. She refused to discuss it over the phone."

"You're going there right now?"

"Yes."

She frowned. "Won't the police think it strange? I mean, your suddenly vanishing after finding Beth's body?"

"They may not like it," he agreed. "But there is nothing criminal in what I propose to do. I'll be available for their questioning when I come back. And, in any case, there's really nothing I can tell them beyond the details of where I discovered the body. Willie will lead them to the spot."

"I suppose you're right."

He started the car. "I'd better drive you back before I go to the clinic."

Suddenly she had an impulse to go with him. "Can I come along? I'm too upset to stay here. I can't bear to think about Beth. And everyone will do nothing but talk about the murder."

Barnabas hesitated. "You're welcome to come along as far as I'm concerned. But what about your mother and your Uncle Roger?"

"I can call the house from here," she said, indicating the pay phone. "We'll not be gone longer than overnight, will we?"

"I'd expect we'll be back by tomorrow afternoon," he said. "Won't you need some clothes?"

"I'll manage," she said. "I expect Dr. Hoffman can supply me with night things."

"You'd better make your call now so we can get started. The clinic is more than a two hour drive from here, and I want to get there before midnight."

Carolyn immediately made the call. She got through to her mother at once and told her, "I'm going to see Dr. Hoffman with Barnabas. We'll be gone overnight."

Her mother sounded near hysteria. "But neither of you should leave at this time!"

"We'll be back tomorrow afternoon. You can let the police know."

"I don't like it at all," Elizabeth protested. "Why is Barnabas going there?"

"He thinks Dr. Hoffman knows something about the murders."

"Then he should tell the police and let them go to her."

Carolyn sighed. "It's confidential information having to do with the clinic. I don't believe she'd be willing to discuss it with the police."

"Why should you become mixed up in it?"

"Because Beth was my friend. I want to find out who is responsible for the murders."

"This will cause talk! You should let Barnabas go alone. Have him drive you home first."

"I'm sorry, mother," she said. "I've made up my mind. I'm going with him. I'll see you tomorrow."

Before her mother could offer any more protests or prolong the argument, she hung up.

Barnabas looked at Carolyn questioningly as she got into the car again.

"Well?" he demanded.

"I told her I was going with you."

"And she didn't approve?"

"No."

He smiled bitterly. "I'm not surprised. And I'm not even sure you ought to make this trip."

Her eyes pleaded with him. "I must. I think it may tell us something about the murders. I want to be there to hear what Dr. Hoffman has to say."

"Very well," Barnabas said quietly, as he started the car.

They were soon on the main highway heading for the village

where Dr. Hoffman's clinic was located. Carolyn knew the pleasant, dark-haired doctor fairly well and she'd also met her associate, portly Professor T. Elliot Stokes. She had been impressed with them both. Now she wondered what they had found out about the murders. She guessed it must have to do with Quentin. As the headlights of the car cut through the darkness in their swaying journey along the curved road, she worried that Quentin might be the killer after all.

Finally she could no longer contain her thoughts. "Barnabas, would you say Dr. Hoffman believes Quentin is involved in the murders?"

"That's difficult to answer," he told her, his eyes on the road ahead. "I'd expect that's the story but I can't be sure. Quentin has been there to seek a cure for his condition. During those spells when he turns into a kind of monster, he's not responsible. It could be she knows of some lapses he might have had which coincided with the killings."

"I hope not."

"So do I. Quentin has his failings, but basically I like him."

"Everyone who really knows him does."

"But if he should be responsible for the murders and Dr. Hoffman has any proof of it, we'll have to turn the information over to the police."

"I realize that. But I'm still betting that the crimes have been Cabrini's work. And if he didn't commit them himself, then Chavez or one of the others associated with him did."

"I agree Cabrini is a major suspect," Barnabas said. "And thanks to him, so am I."

"You mean that attack he complained about to William Kerr? There's no question he put one of those girls up to pretending she'd been the victim of a vampire."

"But William Kerr seemed to believe him and so may the police."

"That's why it's all the more important we learn the truth quickly," she said. Leaning against the seat she closed her eyes and added, "I still can't accept the fact that Beth is dead."

"Try not to think about it."

During the remainder of the drive they spoke little. When they finally reached the clinic and drove into the grounds of the brick-walled estate, the main buildings were in darkness. The only apparent lights were those in one wing devoted to Dr. Hoffman's living quarters.

Barnabas shut off the engine. "They're waiting for us," he said.

He and Carolyn got out of the car and went to the door of the residential wing. Before they could ring the bell, the door opened upon Professor T. Elliot Stokes, who was standing there to greet them.

"Come in," he said genially. "We'd begun to worry that something might have happened to detain you."

"We had a late start," Barnabas told him. "You know Carolyn Collins, I'm sure."

"Of course," Professor Stokes said, his broad face beaming. "We're old friends. Come right in. Julia has a pot of coffee waiting for you."

When they entered the living room. Dr. Hoffman was seated on a divan. A silver tray with a coffee pot, cakes, and cups was in front of her on a low coffee table of chrome and glass. She immediately rose to bid them welcome and offer them refreshment after their long ride.

Only after they were comfortably seated in a semicircle and had been served coffee and the cake did she refer to the reason for their having made the trip.

"I was shocked to hear of the third murder tonight."

Barnabas's handsome face was shadowed. "It was especially shocking to Carolyn since she was a close friend of Beth's and had brought her to Collinsport."

Julia eyed Carolyn sympathetically. "I can well understand your feelings."

Carolyn could contain her fears no longer. "Is Quentin to blame?" she blurted out.

The pleasant woman shook her head. "No. I'm almost positive he isn't. That is why I wanted to talk to Barnabas at once. I have an idea the police may try to blame Quentin. And if he hasn't a strong alibi he could be charged and proven guilty of crimes he didn't commit."

Barnabas said, "Is he in Augusta tonight? Have you any idea where? Can he be reached by phone?"

"I'm sorry," Dr. Hoffman said, "Quentin wouldn't tell me who he was seeing in Augusta. In fact, he slipped away from here without either Dr. Stokes or myself knowing. And that will look bad in the eyes of the police."

"He's done nothing but put himself under suspicion," Barnabas murmured.

Julia nodded. "That's unfortunately true. And I haven't been able to help him as I was able to help you. He is still subject to those spells which make him suspect."

Dr. Stokes spoke up. "I'm not as positive as Julia that Quentin didn't commit the murders. I prefer to reserve an opinion until later."

"I blame Cabrini," Carolyn said rashly. "He's responsible, either directly or indirectly!"

The portly Professor Stokes gazed at her over his coffee cup. "It's interesting you should say that," he said. "Dr. Hoffman has some information for you along that very line."

They all turned to stare at the pleasant, dark-haired woman as she put her cup on the table and sat back against the divan. Her shrewd eyes fixed on Barnabas.

"A few months ago I had an agitated phone call from a wealthy British business man named John Hallam. He happens to be an old friend of mine and he begged me to take on his son, Stephen, for treatment of a mental condition."

Barnabas frowned. "Would that be Hallam of the famous department store on Oxford Street?"

"The same," Dr. Hoffman replied. "I told him he should have the boy put on a plane to Boston. Dr. Stokes met Stephen there and when he brought him here for treatment, I found him to be in a confused mental state, unable to make decisions, or even to think clearly."

"What bearing does Stephen Hallam's treatment have on the murders?" Barnabas asked.

"All in good time," Julia Hoffman said. "In treating Stephen, a good-looking young man of twenty, I discovered he'd been under hypnotic suggestion for months. It was this tampering with his mental powers which had brought him to a breakdown. For some months he'd traveled in England as a member of Cabrini's troupe."

"Cabrini!" Barnabas exclaimed.

"Yes," the woman said. "And in my own hypnotic sessions with Stephen, he revealed truths about those months he'd told no one before. Cabrini had made a slave of him as he does of all his assistants. He reduces them to a state in which they carry out any task he orders."

"I was sure of that," Carolyn said excitedly. "I know his two assistants must be under hypnosis by the way they act!"

"All of his people are," Dr. Hoffman assured her. "But the most startling facts of all were Stephen's revelations of criminal escapades in which he participated, under Cabrini's direction."

Barnabas leaned forward with interest. "That is undoubtedly why the French authorities warned Scotland Yard when Cabrini went to England."

"It could be," Julia agreed. "From what I learned in my sessions with Stephen, he was party to a number of robberies, some involving violence. Cabrini apparently masterminded a series of crimes, following the route his troupe traveled. When they were in Birmingham, a bank was robbed there. In London there were numerous jewel thefts. And in Liverpool a wealthy shipowner was found murdered and his wall safe emptied. All these crimes took place when the Cabrini troupe was in the vicinity. They were undoubtedly perpetrated by his people."

Carolyn said excitedly, "And now they've moved to Collinsport and we have the murders and thefts there. Beth tried to warn me of something the last time I saw her. She was terrified."

Dr. Hoffman shot her a significant glance. "That is probably why she was murdered tonight. To keep her from revealing Cabrini's guilt."

"You may be right," Barnabas said. "What about this Stephen Hallam? Can you produce him as a witness against Cabrini?"

"No," the doctor said unhappily. "About three weeks ago Stephen ran away from the clinic. It is not our custom to keep patients under tight restraints. He took advantage of our trust in him to escape. We haven't been able to locate him, but the police have been notified."

Barnabas frowned. "Do you consider him dangerous? Could he be guilty of the murders and thefts?"

"It's only a slight possibility," Dr. Hoffman said. "I believe he is harmless, though his mind is still confused."

"Not nearly as potentially dangerous as Quentin Collins," Professor Stokes said in his serious manner.

Carolyn said, "The one I really fear is Cabrini. Even if he isn't personally responsible, he plans the crimes."

"That is only supposition," Professor Stokes warned her.

Barnabas glanced at them. "What it amounts to is that we still haven't the proof we need against Cabrini. Now, how can we obtain it?"

"It seems to me the police should pursue their investigations along all lines," Professor Stokes said ponderously. "Eventually they will hit on the solution."

Dr. Hoffman gave her colleague a cynical smile. "I have other ideas." Turning to Carolyn, she told the girl, "I think you might hold the key to the mystery."

"Me?" Carolyn asked in surprise.

"Yes. Because you were close to Beth I think Cabrini will worry that you may have learned something about his criminal activities. I have an idea he'll make you an offer to join his company within the next few days. His plan will be to get you under his power and eventually destroy you."

Barnabas wrinkled his brow. "You believe that?"

"Yes," Julia said. "And the proper action for Carolyn would be to accept his offer; to pretend to be innocent of the danger until she is able to trap him into revealing himself."

"That could be dangerous for her," Barnabas said, glancing at Carolyn.

"Not if she is on the alert and has support from someone else—you, for instance," Julia persisted.

Barnabas sighed. "I don't know."

Carolyn felt it was time to speak for herself. "I think Dr. Hoffman's idea is sound. I can take care of myself and I know the danger. It's the only way we'll ever get evidence against Cabrini."

Barnabas eyed her worriedly. "It will be difficult to make plans without having any idea how he'll approach you."

"We'll have to plan as we go along," Carolyn told him.

From the other end of the semi-circle, the stout Professor Stokes gazed at them with a warning look. "I think you are mistaken in believing Cabrini to be the chief culprit in the Collinsport murders. I still consider Quentin the most likely suspect, and Stephen Hallam a definite possibility."

Dr. Hoffman smiled grimly. "I'm afraid yours is a minority vote, Professor. But I'll gladly eat humble pie if you should be proven right."

"A good deal will depend on the turn events take within the next few days," Barnabas reasoned.

Dr. Hoffman rose from the divan. "And now I think we should all go to bed. It's been a difficult night for us and it looks as though tomorrow won't be any easier."

Carolyn retired to the guest room provided for her and was asleep, from sheer exhaustion, within a few minutes. She slept soundly and late into the morning. By the time she showed up for breakfast Barnabas and Dr. Hoffman had already eaten and gone to the clinic's modern lab.

Carolyn couldn't forget that it was accepted fact that Julia had a deep, personal interest in the handsome, personable Barnabas. Now that she had been successful in restoring him to almost normal health, the chances for a romance between them seemed greater than ever. Yet Carolyn found it hard to dislike this rival for Barnabas's affections, and had an idea that Julia Hoffman was not the sort to press her claim for his love. She would undoubtedly let Barnabas make the choice. And that was all Carolyn could ask.

It was a bleak morning for such ruminations, a heavy fog having descended. Carolyn finished her breakfast and went to the lab to find Barnabas. Dr. Hoffman was leaning over his shoulder as he sat studying some slides under a microscope on her desk.

Julia smiled as Carolyn entered. "You're just in time to see some of the specimens I took of Quentin's blood. It is clear that they differ from ordinary cells."

"I'm sure I wouldn't know, even seeing them," Carolyn said, smiling back.

"If you look at a normal cell slide and then at Quentin's, you'll note the contrast," the doctor assured her.

Barnabas raised his face from the microscope. "Almost time

to drive back," he said, rubbing his neck.

"I know, and I don't look forward to it."

Julia nodded sympathetically. "I understand."

"Still we have to get back," Carolyn said. "So I suppose the sooner we start the better."

She noted that Barnabas gave Julia a casual goodbye kiss on the cheek. It was difficult to tell how devoted they were to each other. She pretended to have no interest. They got in the car and Julia and Professor Stokes waved them on their way.

During the drive back to Collinwood Barnabas seemed strangely preoccupied and silent. It wasn't until they'd nearly reached the ancient mansion that he began to talk a little.

"You don't have to follow through with Julia's suggestion, even if Cabrini does approach you about joining his troupe."

"I know that," she said. "But I want to."

"Don't do it on my account," he warned her. "I can take care of myself."

"I'd be doing it for Beth as much as anyone."

The fog that had followed them along the highway wreathed Collinwood in gray. They could hardly make out the shape of the sprawling mansion until they were upon it.

Barnabas said, "Be careful if the police question you."

"What are you going to do?" Carolyn asked as the car came to a halt.

Barnabas's handsome face was troubled. "First I'm going to try and locate Quentin. That's most urgent. Then I'll have to fend off the police if they come to ask for information."

"When will I see you again?"

"As soon as possible." Barnabas saw that Carolyn was about to protest his vague reply. "I know that's an unsatisfactory answer, but it's the only one I can give you now. I may be going to Augusta or even further in search of Quentin."

She sighed. "I'll be afraid for you every minute of the time."

He gave her a sad smile. "Just look after yourself," he told her, leaning close to kiss her briefly on the lips.

She left the car and he drove off in the fog in the direction of the old house. She watched after the car for a moment and then turned and went inside. The instant she entered the hall, she saw her Uncle Roger standing in the doorway of the living room, an angry expression clouding his face.

"Why didn't Barnabas come in with you and apologize for dragging you off last night?"

"There was no need to. I went with him because I wanted to go."

Her uncle continued to scowl. "You realize that you were

wrong. It was all I could manage to placate the police. As it is they'll be back here to question you and him!"

"That's all right."

"What was the big attraction at Dr. Hoffman's clinic?"

Carolyn said quietly, "Barnabas went there to find out more about Quentin and whether he might be to blame for the murders."

Roger's stern face showed disdain. "No need to go to the clinic to learn that. It's a known fact. Quentin has gone into hiding and the police have a warrant out for him."

"How do you know he's in hiding?"

"He left the clinic and no one can find him," Roger said. "Isn't that proof enough?"

"He may have simply decided to go away for a while."

"A likely story. Even that nuisance, Cabrini, is willing to admit Quentin is the culprit."

"I wouldn't put too much value on what he says."

"The police do," her uncle asserted. "And perhaps you noticed the grounds are in as bad a mess as I predicted from that show!"

"I didn't notice any major damage," she said.

"Or you chose to deliberately close your eyes to it."

"Have the funeral arrangements been made for Beth?"

"Not yet," Roger said. "We're still trying to contact her parents."

"I still can't believe it," Carolyn said, her eyes filling with tears.

Her uncle frowned. "Quentin should have been dealt with long ago. He belongs in an insane asylum."

"How can you blame him so easily when you don't really know he did it?"

Roger eyed her with disgust. "You've been allowing Barnabas to brainwash you."

"No," she said. "I simply happen to believe in Quentin."

"I wouldn't go around making that statement in public," Roger warned her. "You won't be very popular."

"I don't care."

"Barnabas is only a fraction better than Quentin. William Kerr came here early this morning and, among other things, told me that Cabrini claims Barnabas attacked one of his young women."

"That was all a lie," she protested.

"I don't know why Cabrini should be interested in fabricating such a story," Roger insisted.

"Because he wanted to hurt Barnabas."

"Why?"

"For any number of reasons," she said uncertainly. "I'd rather not talk about it now."

"Barnabas told you not to, I suppose."

"What if he did?"

Roger looked resigned. "It's not strange you should be on his side. You've been in his company since Beth's body was discovered last night. No doubt he's attempted to confuse you. And he seems to have succeeded."

"I don't feel like arguing about it," she said. "Where is my mother?"

"In her room. She's very upset. And no wonder."

As Carolyn started up the shadowed stairs, she couldn't help feeling strangely haunted by the memory of Beth. She could almost picture her friend smiling as she stood on the landing, waiting for Carolyn to come up.

She decided to visit her mother's room for a moment and try to set things right about the previous night. But when she reached the room it was empty. Carolyn continued along the dark hallway in the direction of her own room. She had to pass by the room Beth had occupied. Nearing the door, it was as if unseen hands held her back. She hesitated for a moment, but the same strange force compelled her to step up to the door and turn the knob. The door opened easily and she ventured a step into the semi-dark room with its shades partly drawn.

And then she gasped! The rocking chair by the window was in motion!

She stared at it, thinking it might be an optical illusion, but it wasn't. The chair was gently slowing to a halt as she watched it. How many times had she seen Beth rocking in that very chair?

Her eyes wandered to the dresser and she could smell the scent which Beth had used. Moving to the long dresser she noted that the box of face powder was open and the puff, with its sweet odor of perfumed powder, was beside it. Just as if someone had been interrupted in using it.

The familiar setting, the moving chair and the odor of the powder all served to send a cold chill of fear through her. It was as if Beth were there beside her, moving about in the shadows with ghostly invisibility. Suddenly she went rigid as cold fingers touched her bare arm!

CHAPTER 11

Before Carolyn could scream, a hand was around her mouth. Struggling to free herself, she caught a glimpse in the mirror and saw that her captor was not a ghost. It was Quentin!

"Easy," he said in her ear.

She nodded as he released his hold on her, withdrawing his hand from her mouth. She wheeled around to face him. "You terrified me!"

"I had a bad moment when you first came in here," he said. "I was in the chair and made for the closet."

Staring at him anxiously she said, "You know the police are looking for you! You shouldn't be here!"

On his good-looking face appeared a wry smile. "Where would you suggest I go?"

"I don't know," she admitted unhappily. "They think you're the murderer."

His sad eyes met hers. "Can you imagine my killing Beth?"

"No."

"I want to see Barnabas," Quentin said. "Do you know where he is?"

"I just left him," she said. "He'll be at the old house now. He's planning to go in search of you."

"I can save him that trouble."

"Have you any way of proving where you were last night?"

"No. This time I'm in trouble."

"I'm sure that you and Barnabas will think of something," she said.

Quentin smiled. "We'll see. And you'd better watch your nerves. They're in bad shape."

"You haven't helped them," she rebuked him.

"Sorry," he said, taking her in his arms and touching his lips to hers. With one of his teasing looks, he said, "You'd rather it was Barnabas."

"You should be worrying about more serious things," she said, gazing up at him.

"I find that serious enough," he told her. "Now take a look in the hallway and see if the coast is clear."

When she gave him a sign that it was safe to leave the room, he quickly went out and down the hall in the shadows. In a moment he was lost to her view.

She went on to her own room and stretched out on the bed in an attempt to gather her thoughts. The fact that Quentin was lingering in the area complicated things and gave rise to more anxiety in her. Her one hope was that together Barnabas and Quentin would work out some plan against Cabrini.

The next few days were relatively uneventful. She saw no more of Quentin, and Barnabas had gone away on some mission. There was a memorial service for Beth in the village church and, though Cabrini did not attend, Carolyn was pleased to see William and Adele Kerr there.

At the end of the service the white-haired, blind man came to Carolyn and her mother with Adele guiding him. "I'm sick because of what happened to that poor girl," he told Carolyn. "I understand she was your close friend."

"We were like sisters," Carolyn said.

Kerr asked, "Did she ever give you any hint that she considered herself in danger?"

After the sadness of the service, she was in a mood to tell the truth even if it hurt. "Yes," she said, "she did say something to me once about being afraid of Cabrini."

William Kerr looked troubled. "But she chose to live at Kerrhaven and join Cabrini's company. She did those things of her own free will. How do you explain that?"

Carolyn was bitter. "She may have gone there of her own free will, but she didn't remain there because she wanted to. I'm certain he used hypnosis on her. But I told you all that before she was killed, didn't I?"

The blind man sighed. "Yes. I must admit you did. But what can I say? Cabrini has been my friend over the years. I have never known him to do anything wrong."

"Then you mustn't pay attention to what I said," she was quick to tell him. "I'm only offering my point of view."

The old man was leaning heavily on his sister's arm. "But I did ask you for information. I can't blame you. And I promise I'll think about what you told me."

"Let us hope the violence has come to an end," she said bitterly.

"I say amen to that." Adele Kerr finally spoke. "And do come and see us again soon." The two moved on.

When Carolyn and her mother were by themselves once again, her mother asked her, "Weren't you too harsh with that old man?"

"On the contrary," she said. "I felt I was being very considerate, considering that I do believe Cabrini was behind Beth's murder."

Elizabeth looked uneasy. "Now you make me feel responsible. I organized the special show and it happened during the performance."

"More probably, before the performance," Carolyn said as they walked along the street toward their car. "No one seems to be quite sure."

"We'll have to leave it to the police," her mother said. "They don't seem to be accomplishing much."

"If they could find Quentin, they might get a confession," Elizabeth said worriedly. "But I know Roger hopes they don't. He feels it will ruin the family name."

Carolyn's heart pounded faster at her mother's mention of Quentin. "I find a lot of these fears and motives tragically funny," she said. "Of what importance is the family name in a case like this?"

"It is extremely important," Elizabeth said, looking at her daughter sharply.

Carolyn gazed at her mother in disappointment as they reached their car. "You get more like Uncle Roger every day. What concerns me is Quentin's safety and proving that he is innocent."

Her mother stared at her in bewilderment. "Everyone is sure he is guilty."

"And that's the mistake," Carolyn told her mother as she closed the car door after her.

One evening a few days later, Carolyn received a phone call from Kerrhaven.

"I hope you are not angry with me," Cabrini began suavely. "I would have called you before, but not knowing how you felt about me made me hesitate."

"Why have you called?" she asked in a quiet voice.

"I must speak with you," the magician said, "about something that is bothering me. I wondered if you would mind coming over here. It would afford us more privacy."

She knew this was the call Dr. Hoffman had predicted. It was the moment Carolyn had waited for. Now she would pretend to fall for his bait. Everything was falling into place, except that Barnabas was not here to protect her from danger, nor did she have any way of reaching him to notify him of this sudden development. She hadn't any idea where he was. Yet she couldn't turn down this chance. She must risk going along with Cabrini.

She asked, "When do you want me there?"

"Tonight, if you can manage it," Cabrini said with poorly concealed eagerness. "I'll be on the front veranda of the main house, waiting for you."

"I'll be there in half an hour," she said.

"Fine. And it might be wise not to tell anyone of our meeting."

"I understand," she said quietly, amazed that he should believe her to be taken in by his obvious scheme.

It was a pleasantly warm evening and dusk was descending. Carolyn slipped out of the house without her mother or any of the others noticing. First she hurried to the old house on the chance that Barnabas might be there. She couldn't understand what had kept him away so long.

She found Willie Loomis standing on the front steps of the old house and, taking this as a sign Barnabas might be home, hurried up to the youth, full of hope.

"Is Barnabas back?" she asked excitedly.

Willie gave her a cautious look. "No," he said.

"You're sure?"

"Yes."

"Barnabas wouldn't want you to lie to me," she warned him.

"I told you," Willie said indignantly, "he didn't come back."

"Have you any idea when he will be here?"

"He didn't say."

Carolyn was growing impatient with the youth's laconic replies. "Tell him I've been looking for him, if he should come home tonight," she said, trying to sound authoritative.

"All right."

"And if he does come home, say I've gone to Kerrhaven. That Cabrini called and I went to talk to him. Can you remember that?"

"Yes," Willie said with disinterest as Carolyn turned to go.

Carolyn took the car to Kerrhaven. During the drive, she tried to steel herself for the meeting with Cabrini. She didn't know whether or not she could manage to conceal her fear and hatred for him. She surely must make a try, if she was going to trap him into revealing his career of crime. She was certain he was planning to somehow ensure her silence; perhaps he was planning her murder next!

She reached the parking area to which she'd driven so many times with Beth and felt a surge of melancholy in being alone. Her vivacious, pretty friend had always been such good company and now Carolyn would never see her again. Getting out of the car, she hesitantly made her way across the yard to the great mansion which loomed against the darkness. The front veranda on which Cabrini had said he would be waiting, faced the ocean. Strangely, there were few lights showing tonight.

Carolyn almost stumbled in the darkness as she mounted the steps of the side veranda. She moved around to the front of the house, but the veranda seemed to be deserted. Then she heard a board creak behind her and turned to discover the black-clad Cabrini standing there.

"I didn't even see you," she told him, "dressed in black the way you are."

"Wearing black is one of the trade secrets of illusionists," Cabrini said. "When the lights are lowered, it enables one to move about without being seen."

She smiled at him thinly. "You never forget your profession for a moment."

The bald man shrugged. "In Europe we are trained to take our careers very seriously."

"I've gathered that," she said meaningfully.

He motioned her to a wicker chair. "Please sit down."

Her nerves were taut as she asked him, "Why did you invite me here?"

Cabrini stood before her, a lithe figure in black sweater and tights, his arms folded across his chest. "For several reasons. I know you are feeling bad about Beth Mayberry's murder."

"Wouldn't you expect that?"

"Yes," he said. "But I'm upset that you somehow blame me."

"Who told you that?"

"You said as much to my old friend, William Kerr. It created an awkward moment for me."

"I'm sorry," she said. "Perhaps he misunderstood what I was saying."

"I sincerely hope so. I was fond of Beth. I felt she had a great future in my company."

"Indeed?"

"Yes. She was enthusiastic about it, as well," Cabrini went on. "It is a tragedy that your cousin, Quentin, killed her."

"You seem extremely sure of that."

Cabrini spread his hands. "The police are looking for him. Beth's throat was ripped open and that is the way he is said to attack during his madness—what other evidence would you wish?"

"The solid evidence of an eyewitness," Carolyn said firmly.

"I doubt that one is likely to turn up."

"I suppose you also feel that Barnabas is mad, since he allegedly attacked one of your assistants?"

"I feel he is dangerous," Cabrini said with modest correction. "I know of his vampire tendencies and I must say I deplore this strain of decadence in the Collins family. It is all too familiar in most aristocratic families on the decline."

"Not a very flattering picture you paint of my family."

"I assure you I meant nothing personal in my comments," the suave magician said. "You have entirely escaped the taint."

She gazed up at him in the darkness. "You still haven't told me why you asked me to come here."

"I will now." Cabrini sat down beside her so that she could clearly see his striking profile against the sky. "I was greatly impressed by the way you conducted yourself in the show the other night. Now that I have lost Beth, I would like you to take her place."

Even though she had expected something of this sort, she was surprised. "You're asking me to join your company?"

"Yes."

"That would mean living here and rehearsing full time with the troupe?"

"It would," he agreed. "But I'm sure you'd find it a fascinating life."

"You really think I have enough talent?"

"I do."

This was what Dr. Hoffman had predicted, and she knew she should agree as part of their plan to prove the magician's guilt. But she had to pretend reluctance.

"I'm not positive I want to do it."

"I'll make you a star of the show," Cabrini promised, "and you'll have the finest room here in the house."

Carolyn pretended to be considering this, then finally said, "I could try it for a few weeks. If it works out we could make the arrangement permanent."

"Excellent," Cabrini said, clearly delighted. "When can you begin? Can you move in here tomorrow?"

"I suppose so."

"I'll personally attend to all the arrangements, and I'll work out some new routines in which to feature you."

"It will still be on a trial basis," she warned him.

"I understand that," he said, rising, "but I know you're going to like our world well enough to become a permanent addition to it."

Carolyn got up. "I'll have to talk it over with my mother and Uncle Roger. But I feel sure they'll be in favor of the idea."

"Good," Cabrini said. "I consider myself unusually lucky to get a girl with your potential."

He escorted her to her car and warmly bid her goodnight. She drove back to Collinwood with mixed feelings. She was elated that the scheme was working out just as Dr. Hoffman had predicted, but frightened at the danger she would have to expose herself to.

When she reached Collinwood, she put the car away and started across the dark courtyard. She was rounding the old mansion to the front entrance when the caped, erect figure of Barnabas came to her out of the night.

She hurried to meet him. "I'm so glad you're finally back."

"What is wrong?"

She told him of her visit to Kerrhaven. "I'm to go there to live, beginning tomorrow."

"It may be risky."

"I've made up my mind to chance that."

"I'll watch over you as closely as I can," Barnabas promised her.

"It makes all the difference knowing you're back," she agreed happily.

Carolyn stood there in the summer night with him, tense at the knowledge of the dangers she would soon be facing. But she knew she had to go through with the plan, to even the score for Beth.

She asked Barnabas, "What about Quentin?"

"He's gone. He doesn't plan to return until the real murderer is revealed."

He walked her to the front door of the house. When they paused there to say goodnight, she asked him, "Did you find out anything more about Cabrini?"

"No," he said. "I've talked with Julia but she hasn't been able to get any extra information. Nor has Stephen Hallam been found."

She'd almost forgotten about him, she realized. "Isn't it strange he hasn't turned up somewhere?"

"Very," Barnabas said with a deep sigh. "I suspect he's tried to make contact with Cabrini. There has probably been foul play there as well. But there's nothing to prove this as yet."

"I'll leave for Kerrhaven in the afternoon," she told him. "Probably just after lunch. Will I see you before I go?"

"I should be here," Barnabas said. "I'll want to work out some means of keeping contact with you without Cabrini's being aware of it."

"He's doing everything Julia Hoffman said he would."

"She had him measured well," Barnabas agreed. "It will be interesting to know what he'll try next after he has you living at Kerrhaven."

"Only time will tell."

"I'll worry about you," Barnabas said. He kissed her goodnight and sent her inside.

A heavy rainfall and her own fears made the next day full of gloom for Carolyn. At the breakfast table she told Roger and her mother of her intentions.

Her uncle looked at her as if he thought she'd lost her mind. "You're not serious about this, are you?"

"She can't be!" her mother protested. "Why would any girl want to get mixed up with Cabrini after what happened to poor Beth Mayberry?"

"I don't think her murder had anything to do with her being a member of Cabrini's troupe," Carolyn argued. She could not let them think she believed Cabrini to be a murderer if she expected them to give her their blessings in her endeavor.

Elizabeth looked anguished. "It's not a proper life for you, in any event."

"The idea of a Collins joining that charlatan's company is too much!" Roger said angrily. "I've said from the start that William Kerr should never have rented his estate to Cabrini!"

"I agree with you now," Carolyn's mother said. "We've had nothing but trouble since they came here."

"I told you it would be that way," Roger reminded her, "and now it's come home to you." He turned to Carolyn. "I will be greatly disappointed in you if you insist on doing this insane thing."

He tossed his napkin on the table, got up, and angrily strode out of the room.

Elizabeth glanced at her daughter worriedly. "You see how you've upset Roger."

"He upsets too easily."

"He's right about this."

Carolyn shrugged. "I'm sorry. I've made up my mind. I'm moving to Kerrhaven this afternoon." She hoped that her mother wouldn't offer too much resistance to the idea since she knew she would have to go through with the plan in any case.

Elizabeth seemed depressed by the situation but she said nothing more. Carolyn went up to her room and packed her bags. She would leave right after lunch. Now she began to worry about seeing Barnabas.

He arrived shortly after the midday meal. Elizabeth joined him in the hallway to enlist him in an effort to halt Carolyn's plan to move to Kerrhaven.

"Surely she will listen to you, Barnabas. She seems to think Roger and I are unduly prejudiced."

Embarrassed by her mother's words, Carolyn said, "I wish you wouldn't involve Barnabas in this. It's not his concern."

Elizabeth gave her a reproachful glance. "You need advice. I hope he will give you the proper kind." With that she left them together in the living room.

Barnabas watched Carolyn worriedly. "They're pretty upset about your going to Kerrhaven."

"I expected that. But you know I have to go."

"You could back out."

"I don't intend to."

Barnabas turned to stare out the broad living room windows at the rain. "There is something else I should tell you before I let you go to Cabrini."

The gravity of his manner and the fact that he was avoiding looking at her directly sent a small chill through Carolyn. "Something new?"

"Yes."

"Go on."

"This morning Stephen Hallam's body was found at the bottom of the cliffs, not far from Kerrhaven. The verdict will probably be that he killed himself. But I find it difficult to believe that he committed suicide. It's too much of a coincidence that they found him so close to Cabrini's headquarters."

Carolyn's eyes widened with fear. "Of course! Cabrini must have killed him!"

Barnabas turned to fix his serious eyes on her. "I think that's the case. Hallam must have looked Cabrini up. For some reason the magician decided he was a threat and arranged his death to make it seem a suicide."

"Another murder!"

"Yes," Barnabas said in a resigned voice. "And you must realize he'll do the same with you if he thinks it's the only way he can protect himself."

"I still must go there."

"I thought you'd feel that way," Barnabas said, "but I had to warn you."

Driving to Kerrhaven in the rain, Carolyn tried to sustain the courage she would need to face the coming ordeal. She kept her eyes on the road and concentrated on her driving, telling herself not to be afraid. Barnabas had given his promise never to be far from her, but she knew she could only depend on him to a limited extent. If Cabrini decided to murder her, the chances were that he'd succeed. He'd succeeded in all his sinister schemes thus far.

The hunchback, Chavez, met her at the front door of Kerrhaven and carried her bags into the old mansion, which seemed damp and gloomy after the familiar warmth of Collinwood.

"You're to be in the second floor front. I'll take your things up now," Chavez said, as she followed him up the stairs. Her bedroom was pleasant enough. There was a view of the ocean and a private bath. At least Cabrini was keeping his word in giving her excellent accommodations. But she knew this was all part of his scheme to win her over and then destroy her.

"Where is Cabrini?" she asked the hunchback as he was about to leave.

Chavez avoided her eyes. "He's away for a few hours. He'll be back later."

"I'm surprised," she said. "He promised to be here to greet me."

"That's the message he said to give you." Chavez hobbled out and closed the door after him.

The whole atmosphere was such that it made her doubly uneasy. The rain continued as she opened her bags on the large bed to unpack. By keeping herself busy she helped hold her nerves in check. She wondered why Cabrini wasn't there, and what had happened to make him leave so unexpectedly—if he had indeed left! Perhaps he was lurking somewhere in the house and this was merely part of his scheme to undermine her resistance.

After she unpacked, Carolyn stretched out on the bed and tried to rest. She had no idea how long she'd been asleep when she was awakened by a light knock on her door. She looked up to see Chavez come in with a tray.

"Your dinner," he said, putting the silver tray on a table by the window, then quickly turning to go.

Carolyn was puzzled by what was happening. Why was she being served in her room? She forced herself to eat a little of the meat and vegetables, and drank the coffee. Then she waited.

The rain ended in a drizzle and soon dusk settled. From distant parts of the house she occasionally heard muffled voices, but no one came to her. Not even Chavez to get the tray. She began to pace up and down uneasily as the night progressed. Suddenly, there was another knock on her door.

She opened it to find Cabrini standing imperiously in his black sweater and tights. There was a mocking smile on his bony face. "Have you been made comfortable?"

"Yes," Carolyn said, "But I've been wondering where you were."

Cabrini entered the room. "I'm sorry I wasn't able to give you my attention until now," he said. "I had some pressing matters to attend to."

"I see," she said coolly.

"Now I'd like to show you some of the rest of the house," the magician told her. "Especially a room in the attic which I'm using as an extra rehearsal area."

"Wouldn't it be better to wait until morning?" she asked, sensing something menacing in his manner.

He shook his head and took her by the arm. "No, I insist that you come with me now."

Feeling the tight grasp of his fingers on her arm as he led her into the hallway, realizing that she was completely alone with him and isolated from all help in this old mansion, Carolyn suddenly felt—like a prisoner!

CHAPTER 12

Cabrini pushed Carolyn toward the stairway, saying, "We go up this way."

Carolyn would have shown more resistance under normal circumstances. But she was deliberately seeing how far the magician was prepared to go. They mounted two flights of shabby stairs, after which he led her down a dark, narrow hall to a door that was partly ajar.

Cabrini guided Carolyn into a large room draped entirely in red curtains. There were no windows of any sort and in each corner of the room torches burned in metal stands.

She stared around her as Cabrini closed the door. Turning to him, Carolyn said, "You've certainly created a strange atmosphere in here."

Cabrini smiled mysteriously. "There is a reason," he said, walking to a table draped in black which stood in the middle of the room. He removed the black covering to reveal a crystal ball, which seemed to be illuminated from below.

Carolyn said, "I've never seen you use a crystal ball in your magic."

"I sometimes do some illusions with it," Cabrini told her. "But mostly I use it as an aid in hypnotism."

She was at once on the alert. "I see," she said calmly.

The glow of the crystal ball touched his bony face as the magician stood over it. His burning, deep-set eyes fixed on Carolyn's as he told her, "I now propose to send you into a hypnotic trance. It will be part of your training here."

"No!" she protested. "I don't want to be hypnotized."

Cabrini looked coldly amused. "I'm afraid you are going to be whether you wish it or not."

Carolyn drew back and moved toward the door. As she did, it opened and Chavez took a position to block her escape. She turned to appeal to Cabrini. "I'm willing to cooperate in any way but I don't want to be hypnotized."

The bald man was studying her with cold triumph. "Surely you didn't take me for such a fool as to believe you had come here to join my company. I know why you're here. To get evidence against me; to try and prove that I'm the one responsible for the murders."

"No!" she protested, cold fear gripping her.

Cabrini came close to her, his eyes boring into hers. "You needn't lie! I know what you think of me! Beth told me when I had her under hypnotism. Tonight I'm going to place you under my control, and at my command are going to take your own life. Then no one will suspect me!"

"There'll be Barnabas!"

"Barnabas!" the magician said with contempt. "I know how to take care of him. There are going to be more attacks against young women of the village and the clues will all lead to Barnabas. Before I'm finished he'll be driven out of the area."

"You are the one then," she said, her pretty face pale with fear. "You engineered all the murders!"

"Murders? But you'll just be another suicide, Miss Collins," Cabrini said, seizing her arm again. "No one will suspect me!"

"They're bound to!" she gasped, trying to free herself from his grip.

"I'm perfectly safe," Cabrini gloated. "People know you were shocked by Beth's murder and that you've been moody ever since. They'll believe that you were in exactly the right frame of mind to commit suicide."

Carolyn knew that what he was saying was true. If he managed to hypnotize her and turn her into one of his living puppets, he could order her to do anything and she would obey him mindlessly. All he required was the influence of his burning, evil eyes to break her will! "You're mad!" she cried.

"If I'm mad, it's extremely rewarding," he told her, laughing maniacally. Then he fixed his gaze on her.

She averted her eyes, but she knew that she'd been trapped. There was no hope, no use in screaming or fighting. It was too late for that. She would die like Cabrini's countless other victims and no one would suspect him.

Cabrini shook her roughly and tried to make her look at his face. "No use being stubborn," he warned her.

She turned her head again, knowing she couldn't fight him off much longer. Then as she glanced toward the hunchback at the door, she thought she saw the door slowly opening. The glowing red torches against the walls of red velvet curtains had created a confusing, shadowy atmosphere. It might well be an illusion.

But now the door swung all the way open and Barnabas was there. Silently he lifted his walking stick and brought it down full force on Chavez's head. The hunchback uttered a groan and slumped to the floor.

"You!" Cabrini cried. Letting go of Carolyn, he grabbed one of the flaming torches from its stand and held it like a weapon, high above his head, as he advanced to meet Barnabas. As the two men came together Carolyn drew back to the velvet draped wall.

With a sudden, swift motion, Cabrini swung the torch down to strike Barnabas across the face.

As Carolyn screamed, Barnabas parried the flaming torch with his cane. The agile Cabrini came at him again with the torch and this time the flames touched Barnabas's shoulder as he leaped aside.

Dropping the cane, Barnabas dove forward to grasp Cabrini. The magician let the torch fall from his hand as he sought to combat Barnabas. The torch rolled across the floor and its flame touched the red velvet curtains. Before Carolyn could kick the torch aside, the drapes were burning wildly.

In the center of the room, the two men continued to rock back and forth in desperate battle. Cabrini was thin and strong but Barnabas was his equal in strength if not quite as fast. The room was becoming a blazing inferno. The curtains were on fire all around them.

Smoke made Carolyn choke and her eyes filled with tears. Then she saw Barnabas deliver a crushing body blow to the magician, followed by a direct thrust to Cabrini's jaw which sent him to the floor in a crumpled heap. Barnabas immediately turned to Carolyn and guided her out of the smoke and flame-filled room. Smoke was filling the hallway but they made their way downstairs. Left behind in the burning room were the two unconscious men.

Now the alarm quickly sounded through the old mansion. The company of assistants went running wildly from the house, clutching their personal possessions. Flames had already begun to shoot up through the roof from the attic room. It was plain that Kerrhaven was doomed.

Barnabas's face was bleeding and he was breathing heavily as he stood on the lawn with Carolyn, watching the house being consumed by fire. Cabrini's foreign assistants were shouting back and forth in their own language and there was general pandemonium and panic.

Carolyn felt ill. She leaned against Barnabas for support as she asked him, "What about Chavez and Cabrini?"

His handsome face was grim, his dark hair in wild disarray. "I don't think there's any chance for them. They'll never get out of that room alive. And we couldn't have gone back in to get them. The fire spread too quickly."

She saw that the entire second and third floors were a mass of flames. The crackling and roaring filled her ears and the heat was intense even at a distance. No, she thought, there was no hope for the two doomed men.

"They deserved to die," she said in an awed tone, thinking aloud.'

"Certainly Cabrini brought on his own destruction," Barnabas said. "I'd better get you back to Collinwood."

"What about the Kerrs?" Carolyn asked as they walked to the parking area.

Barnabas glanced in the direction of the cottage. "They're all right. The fire won't travel that way."

"The people in the village will see the flames and send the volunteer fire department," she said.

"I imagine so," Barnabas agreed, "but I'd like to get you back to your home before they panic at the idea of your being caught in the fire."

The drive to Collinwood took only a few minutes. From the front door of the great mansion the flames of Kerrhaven were clearly visible, high in the dark sky. The fire would undoubtedly be seen for miles up and down the coast.

Elizabeth came to the door with Roger as Carolyn and Barnabas approached, and threw her arms around her daughter.

"Thank goodness you're safe," she said brokenly.

"Barnabas rescued me," Carolyn told her mother.

Roger stared at the distant flames, his face grim. "What started the blaze?"

"Cabrini dropped a burning torch and it ignited some curtains," Barnabas told him. "The place is so old and dry that the flames spread like wildfire."

"Is he in there?"

Barnabas nodded gravely. "He was when we last saw him. Both he and his assistant, Chavez, were caught in the blaze."

"One way or another it should be the last of the company," Roger said grimly. "They'll have to move on, with Kerrhaven in ashes."

By the dawn of the following morning, the mansion had been reduced to smoking rubble. Only the outbuildings and the cottage had been saved. The dozen or more members of Cabrini's troupe stood around in dull-eyed shock, having saved little more than the clothes on their backs. Cabrini and Chavez were missing, as was one of the girl assistants. Although the ashes would be searched for their bodies, Collinsport lacked the personnel to do the job quickly. It might be days or even weeks before the bodies were found.

It was late the next day when Adele Kerr drove up to the front door of Collinwood with her blind brother. Elizabeth welcomed them inside, where they sat and told their version of the night's blaze.

"We were wakened by the intense light of the flames," Adele said.

White-haired William Kerr sat slumped in an easy chair, looking shattered. "A most calamitous affair," he mourned. "Three lives lost in the flames and one of the dead my friend, Cabrini. And Kerrhaven destroyed! A fine building which can never be reproduced." The face behind the dark glasses took on a slight frown. "There is talk that there was a fight between Barnabas and Cabrini in the attic of the house, and that that was where the fire started. Can you tell us about it, Carolyn?"

Carolyn felt ashamed. She glanced at the blind man and said, "It was Cabrini's fault. He was trying to keep me there against my will. Barnabas came to my rescue and Cabrini threatened him with a flaming torch. There was a struggle and the curtains in the room caught fire."

William Kerr looked haggard. "I knew it had to be something like that. From what you say, Cabrini was in the wrong."

"He surely was," Carolyn said, glad that only she and her mother were there with the two visitors. She could more easily tell the facts, without interruptions from Roger.

Adele Kerr spoke up. "We are going to see that the members of the company are given something to cover their losses and pay their fares back to their homes."

"That is most generous of you," Elizabeth said.

"We have the money," William Kerr told her. "I think it is a good way to spend it."

"I agree," Carolyn said. "You'll be helping those people a great deal."

"So the estate will be rid of all of them within a few days," Kerr promised. "Adele and I will go on living in the cottage. In a way, it's a relief not having the big house to look after."

"We made a terrible mistake in renting to Cabrini," Adele mourned.

Her brother sighed. "How could I have been so wrong about

his character? He was a villain after all."

Carolyn said, "I'm afraid so, but he's gone now."

"Yes, no point in talking about the dead," William Kerr said. "I feel the entire chapter should be closed. Where is Barnabas?"

"I expect he's at the old house," Carolyn said.

"An interesting person," Kerr said. "I must say he proved capable of dealing with Cabrini when all the rest of us had failed."

"He's a competent and talented person," Carolyn agreed.

Adele Kerr smiled at her. "You must come and visit us more often. William likes to be read to, but he gets tired of listening to my voice. I'm sure he'd enjoy having you come over and read to him."

"I'll keep that in mind."

Because the Kerrs were in such a forlorn mental state following the fire, Carolyn made it a point to call on them every afternoon. William Kerr soon had her reading to him from his favorite books and she thoroughly enjoyed the experience.

Barnabas was still at the old house. He frequently came to visit Carolyn in the evenings. One dusk when they were walking along the cliffs, he told her, "The last of Cabrini's vans left today. None of his people are still here."

She gave a shudder. "It all seems like a bad dream now that it's over."

"It was real enough," he assured her. "Real enough to lead to murder and destruction. But perhaps we should think of it only as a bad dream that's finally come to an end."

"Have you heard from Quentin?" Carolyn asked as they came to Widows' Hill.

Barnabas halted and gazed out at the ocean. "No," he said. "He's probably decided to keep traveling, even though the police are no longer looking for him."

She sighed. "My statement seemed to be all that was needed to clear him. I'm glad Cabrini confessed the murders to me before he died."

"It's too bad Quentin doesn't know about that."

"And there's no way of telling him—we have no idea where he is."

"I'm sure I'll run into him sooner or later," Barnabas said, gazing into Carolyn's eyes.

She tried to read the expression on his handsome face, but the night was too dark. "Are you going away, too?"

"In a week or so."

"I hoped you'd remain here this time."

"I get restless," he said. "I have to move around."

"But thanks to Julia Hoffman you're well again. Why not remain here and live a normal life?"

Barnabas stared sadly at the distant ocean. When he spoke it was in a thoughtful voice. "I've been to the clinic several times since the fire. Julia has made dozens of tests of my blood, and she fears the cells are gradually changing. In a few weeks I could know that awful thirst again."

Carolyn was stunned. "I don't believe it!"

"I don't want to, either," he said. "But Julia is worried and I have great confidence in her ability as a doctor."

"Isn't there anything she can do to prevent the change in your blood?"

"She's trying several serums. But we won't know their effectiveness for a while."

"No matter what happens, you can remain here. You'll have Willie to guard you. And me as well, if you marry me."

Barnabas turned to her with an unhappy smile. "Am I to seriously regard that as a proposal?"

"Yes."

"It's most flattering."

"You need me, Barnabas," Carolyn persisted, "and I'm in love with you. You know that."

He took her hand tenderly in his. "Of course I know it. But do you think I'd allow you to marry me when there's this terrible possibility of my becoming a creature of the night again?"

"We've been through that. I know how it is and I can live with it."

His eyes met hers. "You think that now, but later when you face the full horror of it, you might change your mind."

"Never!"

"We must be patient," Barnabas insisted. "We must wait."

"You'll go off alone and I won't know whether you're well or sick."

"You can always find out from Julia."

She gave him a questioning look. "Are you in love with her? And if you are, why don't you marry her? She has been able to help you."

Barnabas smiled sadly. "I don't love Julia, though I like and admire her."

Carolyn gave a deep sigh. "It will be the same as always. One evening I'll go to the old house to find you, and you'll have gone."

"It's probably better that way," he said. "Partings can be painful."

"So can living alone."

"It's time you did something about that," Barnabas said. "There are plenty of young men around who'd be glad to have such a pretty wife."

"I'm not interested in them," she said. "Not as long as I have a chance with you."

"We'll talk about it later." He drew her close to him for a lasting kiss, but even as she relaxed in his arms, she knew that he would probably always avoid speaking of marriage.

A few days later she sought him out to tell him of an offer she had received, hoping that he might be moved to make a decision about their future together. She found him at the old house and, as they sat in the living room, she revealed her news.

"I was over reading to William Kerr today," she began.

Barnabas was interested. "You go over there a lot, don't you?"

"I have, since the fire. They're so lonely. And today they asked me to travel to London with them for the fall and winter." She paused. "So maybe my life isn't going to be so dull after all."

"I told you that."

"Mother is willing to let me go. In fact she's pleased."

"It sounds like a marvelous opportunity," Barnabas agreed. "Where do the Kerrs live in London?"

"They have a town house in Doringham Square, number twelve," she said. "They must be fabulously wealthy. They plan to return here in the spring, and I could come back with them. Of course, you know I'd rather stay here and marry you. But if you must be stubborn..."

Barnabas smiled indulgently, but made no comment.

"What do you think I should do?" she asked at last.

"It's hard to say. I would like to go over and see William Kerr some evening. I haven't been over there since the night of the fire."

"Why not go this evening?" she suggested. "They are always home and happy to have company. They beg me to return each day."

"Shouldn't you ask them first?"

"It's not necessary," she said. "They often inquire about you. I'm sure they feel friendly toward you."

"Very well," Barnabas said. "We'll go over there around eight."

The summer evenings were getting shorter now that August had arrived. Carolyn and Barnabas decided to walk over to the cottage, and by the time they reached it darkness was at hand. Lights blazed cheerfully from the cottage windows and Carolyn looked forward to a pleasant evening of hearing Barnabas and the Kerrs talk about London.

Adele Kerr welcomed them at the door. She seemed a little surprised to see Barnabas, but invited them in at once. A few minutes later, the white-haired man came groping his way into the living room to join them.

The lined face behind the black glasses showed a smile as he sat down with them. "What a wonderful idea of Carolyn's to bring you here," he told Barnabas.

"I've heard about your generous offer to take her to London."

"We're hoping she'll accept," Adele said. "Please try to convince her she should, Mr. Collins."

"It sounds like a fine opportunity for her," Barnabas said. "She's told me that you have a home in Doringham Square."

"Yes," Kerr said, "number twelve."

Barnabas was staring at the Kerrs oddly. "That's strange," he said.

"What is strange?" William Kerr asked.

"I'm well acquainted with Doringham Square," Barnabas told him, "and I happen to know there is an art museum at number twelve."

There was a moment of strained silence. Carolyn glanced around, feeling ill at ease but not knowing what to make of it. Adele seemed stunned, while William Kerr had gone pale and was sitting very still. Barnabas was staring intently at the white-haired man.

At last Kerr spoke. "I think you must be in error, Mr. Collins," he said. "Number twelve is our home."

"Indeed," Barnabas said. "Then it must have become a headquarters for magic." As he spoke, he sprang up from his chair and ran over to the blind man. In one quick movement he snatched the black glasses from William Kerr's face and with his other hand pulled the white wig from his head. Revealed were the familiar features of Cabrini!

"It can't be!" Carolyn cried out.

"I should have guessed earlier," Barnabas said. "This was a convenient out for you, Cabrini. You'd arranged it all carefully in advance: A second identity to assume, should Cabrini's murders and robberies ever be uncovered."

Cabrini smiled coldly. "Good deduction, Mr. Collins."

Barnabas turned to Adele, who stood with her hands nervously clasped. "And this, undoubtedly, is your wife— and not your sister."

"You are remarkably perceptive," Cabrini said, suddenly producing a gun from his jacket pocket. "But not quite perceptive enough!" As he spoke he fired the gun at Barnabas, who staggered backwards and collapsed.

In the next instant Cabrini was out of the cottage and racing across the lawn to the parking area, with Adele following. Carolyn fell to her knees beside Barnabas, trying to stop the flow of blood from his shoulder. At last his eyelids opened and he raised himself up a little. "A shoulder wound," he said. "I'll be all right."

"He could have killed you!" Carolyn sobbed. Barnabas struggled to his feet. He looked pale, on the point of collapse.

"Call the State Police," he told Carolyn. "Tell them to watch for a car heading from here toward the main road."

She nodded. "I will. Is it safe to leave you? Are you sure you're all right?"

"Yes. But you'd better hurry."

She ran to the next room and made the call. By the time she returned, Barnabas had managed to make his way outside. He was standing by the door with Adele.

He told Carolyn, "She's agreed not to make any trouble. She knows it's the end of Cabrini's games." Carolyn gave the elderly woman a look that was full of pity, then turned to Barnabas. "I'm more concerned about you right now," she said. "I'm taking you to the village to see the doctor."

She helped him to the car and Adele came along to sit bleak-faced and silent in the rear seat as they drove through the darkness. At the intersection with the main highway, they came upon the red lights and screaming sirens of a police block. Ahead on the right were a car and a truck in a ditch, both ablaze.

Carolyn brought her car quickly to a halt as a state trooper came running up to them. He recognized her at once. "That fellow you phoned us about came onto the highway at maybe a hundred miles an hour and ran into an oil truck."

From the rear seat came a strangled moan. Barnabas glanced at Adele, then asked the trooper. "How about the drivers of the car and truck?"

"Fellow in the car is still in there. He's a goner. The truck driver came out of it all right, though."

Barnabas nodded grimly. "The man in the car was Cabrini."

"That's what Miss Stoddard said on the phone," the state trooper told him. "We thought he had died in the Kerrhaven fire."

"It's a long story," Carolyn said anxiously. "I haven't time to tell it now. Barnabas has been wounded. I've got to get him to a doctor."

The trooper was staring at the bloodstained cape. "You're not joking," he gasped. "I'll have one of our boys lead the way. We don't want any more accidents tonight."

A few minutes later Carolyn was speeding the car along the road to Collinsport with a police car in front, its siren screaming. Barnabas sat quietly, weak from his loss of blood.

Carolyn gave him a quick glance and the sight of his drawn, gaunt face filled her with anxiety. "After tonight there can be no question. You mustn't ever leave me."

"When have I ever wanted to?" Barnabas asked.

The sadness in his voice pierced her heart. She knew that at this moment he meant it, yet she was just as sure that he would recover and one day she'd find him gone. All her loneliness would return once more. The siren wailed mournfully as she drove on through the night.